PRAISE FOR *TO BRING MY SHADOW*

"Phillips gets better with each book, using crime as a vehicle to penetrate the depths of the human soul..."

—Travis Richardson, Derringer winner
and author of *Bloodshot & Bruised*

"An outstanding hardboiled police thriller full of intrigue, corruption, murder, existential dilemmas, and more. One of the best and most prolific contemporary authors working—make room on your bookshelf for Frank Pinson and Slade Ryerson."

—Andrew Davie, author of
Pavement and *Ouroboros*

"In *To Bring My Shadow,* Phillips treats readers to the down-and-dirtiest whodunnit they'll ever read. Let's be clear: this ain't no tea-cozy and hardboiled doesn't quite cut it, either. Some of the central tropes are Tarantinoesque and Phillips' dialog and eye for detail bring to mind *The Wire.* But this is something else—something *unclean*, cheeky and fun. Have a go."

—Steve Lambert, author of *Philisteens*

"Relentless, gritty, and heart-pounding... An authentic portrayal of San Diego, fantastic characterization, and Phillips' sharp-as-a-knife writing skill make this a must-read."

—Curtis Ippolito, author of
Burying The Newspaper Man

TO BRING MY SHADOW

BOOKS BY MATT PHILLIPS

MATT PHILLIPS

TO BRING MY SHADOW

All Due Respect Books
an imprint of Down & Out Books
3959 Van Dyke Road, Suite 265
Lutz, FL 33558
DownAndOutBooks.com

Cover design by Math Bird

ISBN: 1-64396-222-1
ISBN-13: 978-1-64396-222-1

Part One

Chapter 1

I was drunk the night we caught the Castaneda case. Not too drunk, okay, but blitzed enough to ask Slade if he wanted to do the driving. When the call came in, I was staring at a hole in my bathroom floor. In one hand, I held a glass of mezcal and, in the other hand, a rusted monkey wrench. The dim light from the bathroom's lone bulb gave everything a vague yellowish tint, like I was seeing the world from a different dimension.

But why the hole in the floor?

In the hall, wrapped in cellophane and cardboard, I had a new toilet to install, an American Standard. Picked it up from the hardware store after work. The old shitter, with its rubbed-off brand name and chipped porcelain, sat to one side, next to the tub. It was still dirty from six months of my morning routine.

Uncleaned. Tarnished.

I'll admit it: When Miranda died, I let our little house go to absolute hell. At forty-nine years old, I was a lazy housekeeper, a mal-practicing Catholic, and a widower with only my own denial keeping me from being officially declared a drunk.

Don't worry—the detective knows he's a cliché.

It's funny what death can do to somebody. It doesn't matter what side you're on—you could be a cop or a crook, but death will sink her teeth into you like a ragged mutt on a Tijuana street.

My wife was dead. And I was depressed.

Maybe I was a lazy housekeeper, but I worked my ass off at the old day job. And had been working my ass off for more than twenty years. My shitter was filthy—so what?

My phone chirped again. I dropped the monkey wrench—it clanged like hell—and pulled my cell from my pleated slacks. Yes, unwashed and un-ironed since Miranda got put in the ground. Best I could tell, I'd been through my entire wardrobe six times since her funeral. Surprising how often you can wear a shirt if you're careful with the salsa in your tacos. Or, in my case, if you ate less and less. I knew the call was from Slade, so I didn't bother with formality. "Yeah?"

"Frank, it's me." Slade's voice came across the line like cotton through a straw. Man was probably half asleep, calling from the landline he insisted on keeping. Slade slept like an alligator—he didn't need Mexican medicine. Not like I did.

"What's going on, Slade? We catch a body?"

"Under the bay bridge. Street cop said to bring a cigar or two."

"Rotten meat, huh?" I stared into the black hole in my bathroom floor.

Slade cleared his throat and said, "I get the impression it'll kill your hard-on, Frank."

I grunted, choked down some mezcal. The hole gaped at me, black as a crow's eye. "You get any info from the guy, about the scene or whatever?"

"You mean a pithy summation of the young man's police work?"

"Like that, yes." Slade had his way with the dictionary, or thesaurus. He had some college.

Slade took a long breath, chirped his lips, and said, "Sounds like we got a dead guy found his way into an oil drum."

"Now," I said, "how in the hell did that happen? What was he doing in there, trying to find a heads-up penny?"

"Could be it," Slade said. "I guess I wonder why he cut off his own fingers with bolt-cutters though. Kind of hard to pick up pennies when you don't have fingertips. You think maybe he cut off his dick so he didn't have to piss in the barrel?"

"Jesus H. They cut off the guy's junk?"

"What I heard from the street cop. Heard, too—they're still trying to find it."

"What?"

"The guy's Johnson." Slade chuckled. He was shaking off his slumber.

I sighed from the swell of my belly up through my throat. The last thing I wanted was a whodunit drug murder down in the barrio. Another swim in the deep end for me and Slade, that's what it sounded like. "Maybe we call the guy a homicide, but file a missing person's report for the junk."

Slade gasped. I could hear him working that one through, sitting there in his jammies. "But the guy is there. And the junk isn't another person, is it? I mean, shit, we got the guy. I never heard of a search for a dude's junk. Not that I can remember."

"My junk," I said, "ain't never had trouble being

5

found." I moved toward the black hole, unzipped my pants. I gulped the last of my mezcal, set the glass on the toothpaste-spotted vanity. Miranda wanted me to replace that, too. And the old porcelain tub. And the Mexican tile in the kitchen. "You mind driving tonight, Skinny? I loosened a few screws when I got home."

"I'll be over there in about ten minutes. Hey, you pick up that new shitter?"

"I'm staring at a black hole in my bathroom floor."

"Another project that'll have to wait."

I said, "Like making the world a better place, huh?"

"That's a job that'll never finish."

I wedged the phone between my shoulder and cheek, whipped out my junk and pissed straight down the throat of the black hole. "Say, Skinny, you ever sit around and wonder…Are we pissing this life down the fucking drain?"

Slade hung up without responding.

Chapter 2

Slade "Skinny" Ryerson had a criminal justice degree from an HBCU back east. Tiny college with a long name I never remembered. Man came out west for his juris doctorate, but along the way he got snagged for police work, found himself patting crooks on the back with a nightstick. Slade was too smart to be a cop—first thing he knew, an old school commander made him take the detective examination. Four years in and Slade Ryerson moved his badge from over his heart to a chain dangling around his neck. Became a stone-cold murder police.

Like me. A homicide detective.

Slade pretended—though he didn't admit it—that he was a movie star cop. You know the type: Dude wore a black leather jacket, faded at the elbows. Had himself a nice set of expensive shades, a spare pistol—one of those .25s the movie star girls carry in their purses—tucked slim and sweet in an ankle holster. Left leg, always. The man sauntered like Denzel Washington, eye-fucked gangbangers while I smoked cigars and thought about my pension. Slade was fifteen years my junior and had a lot to learn about the human capacity for cruelty, murder and death. He smiled too damn much.

But when it came to being a cop, I was the immature one.

On this August night—clear, but with a hot breeze—Slade slid the black department-issued Ford Focus (fucking budget cuts) to the curb outside my house. This was what passed for undercover in our city. Fix Or Repair Daily, just like my soggy melon of a brain. Through the tinted passenger window, I made out Slade's widow's peak shining like a vampire fang. Slade never went anywhere without his hair slicked back, those precious black locks coated in Murray's-brand pomade. Did I mention Slade was a ladies' man?

I opened the door and got in, ignored the seat belt. "Thanks for the ride, partner."

"You sober enough for this?" Slade slid his dark eyes over my face. I could feel his brain firing judgment down into his throat, but he knew what I'd been through. He knew how it went down with Miranda, my son and daughter, the life insurance policy. And my own sweet, precious little detective's heart. Slade knew about the burn running through me, the fire, and he kept his righteous remarks to himself. That's why me and Slade got along, how we did the job so damn well. "If you're not sober," Slade said, "we can stop for coffee and some eggs. Trust me, the dead don't hurry, if you know what I mean."

I cleared my throat and said, "I could use a snort of tequila. Hit that dive bar down off—"

"Coffee, Frank. We got a case to work." Slade shifted into drive and the compact car accelerated, a rattle coming from somewhere under the dented hood.

Slade drank too. Don't think he didn't. But Slade knew when to stop. Hell, he had a knack for how to

8

stop. Not me. I'd put one drink down the gullet and I'd already have the second one ordered. The third would be waiting for me by the time I started the second. That way my whole life. If you asked me to be honest, I'd say it hurt me not to drink. It hurt me to be healthy. Sure, I was killing my body. But I was keeping myself alive.

"Shit," I said. "Coffee will have to do then."

Slade turned east on Market, drove for a few blocks and pulled into an empty parking lot. I lurched into a rundown McDonald's for some cheap coffee. We lived in a coffee city, whatever that is, but most cops wear their taste buds through after a year or two. It's the midnight shift that does it, all that 7-Eleven coffee and the bitter taste of human deviance. You're a cop for a few years and the whole world starts to taste like hell. It's pitiful when you say it like that, but here's something to remember: a lot of us like that taste.

When I got back to the car, Slade's cell was pressed to his ear and his brow was crushed down toward his jagged nose. He grunted once, whistled a high note.

"What is it?" I said, handing him a coffee.

He took the coffee with one hand, waved me off with the other. "What do I think it means? Hell if I know. I'll run it by Frank, see what he says. I guess it could be a cartel thing. Or, shit, maybe he upset a pretty little lady somewhere. Sounds like something a lady—"

A voice cut him off, droned on for a minute.

"I'm not saying a lady did the guy," Slade said. "Only that it could have been—"

Slade slumped back in his seat while the voice interjected. He sipped from his coffee while the lecture burned across the line. After a minute or two, Slade pressed the red end call button on his cell, tossed it into

9

one of the cupholders in the center console.

"Crime techs are on scene, huh?" I smirked at my coffee, sipped. There it is, I thought, that hellish bitter taste. "Those fuckers already telling us how to do our job?"

Slade said, "They found the guy's junk."

"You mean his Johnson?"

"Yes, Frank."

"And?"

Slade sighed, got that world-weary look on his face: fucking eyebrows drawn down into a V, his chin all wrinkled like a baby on the verge of crying. "And, they found it in a pickle jar, floating beneath the bridge. The jar was half-full with piss."

A yellowish tint, I thought. My turn to whistle. "Kudos to the techs," I said. "Good find, man: some guy's Johnson bobbing out there in the bay like a message in a bottle. Like searching for a needle in a...well, you get my meaning. You think it's the guy's piss?"

"Possibly."

"Can't rule it out," I said. "Take a wee-wee and chop off your weener—can't say I ain't seen worse."

"Nope, sure can't." Slade started the car, slid us into the empty street. He made an illegal U-turn and headed west, toward the sea.

Ahead, on the horizon, I made out the flared hump of the Coronado Bay Bridge cutting through the sea mist, yellow-orange lights spanning its length. The bridge ran for a mile across the open bay, landed on Coronado Island. Different jurisdiction over there—the island had its own PD.

I wondered aloud: "They found the Johnson on our side of the bay?"

Slade grunted. "You got it."

"No jurisdiction issues then," I said.

"It's all ours, Frank. You and me and the weener makes three." Slade loosed the half-hearted laugh of a tired detective. Hollow. Less than melodic.

"The case of the missing weener," I said. "How sweet is that?"

Ahead, in the soft glow of the midnight horizon, the bridge rose above us like an inverted smile.

Chapter 3

We stood beneath the bridge, right where it took flight over the bay and curved toward the distant shape of Coronado Island. Beside us, a barrier of jetty rocks stretched down into the black, lapping water. I imagined an audience of spotted bay bass watching, their fine-toothed mouths opening and closing like giant pupils. The hot wind somehow blew a chill through me. I took notice of the shipyard to the south, a smattering of warehouses to the north. We were standing in a kind of no-man's-land, an access point to the bay that was likely unregulated. The city was responsible for it, but I doubted any maintenance team had been here in the last couple years. Everything was bathed in yellow from the security lights that lined the chain-link around the shipyard. I saw a security guard lingering beside the fence, one hand dangling on the fence, the other waving a flashlight in aimless boredom. I said, "Might have seen something."

Slade was sketching in his notebook. He eyeballed the security guard and squinted. "Could be. Or maybe just a looky-loo on the midnight shift. You know how it is."

A crime scene tech who appeared too young to grow

a beard approached in his yellow windbreaker. "Detective Pinson, Ryerson. We got a homicide here—brutal, as you might imagine—and a detached, eh, penis along with some missing fingertips and—"

"Slow it down for me, pal." I said. "I'm an old motherfucker and I need to write this shit down, okay?" The tech nodded, watched my callused hand as I swept half a pencil across a tiny notebook.

He said, "The way those fingers came off, through and through, bone flat, I can guess it's something sharp. But it looks like a hand tool from the way the skin and tendons tore at the bottom. I can see—"

"What are you, the fucking coroner?"

The kid frowned, adjusted the flapping collar on his lab coat. "You know, you dicks are all the same. Too fucking worried about jokes to—"

"Keep your complaints to yourself. Nobody gives two fat shits. Let me do the thinking."

The tech shrugged, sighed. "Fine. So, the guy is folded up, like a doll, and he's shoved into the oil drum. I mean, shit..."

"You got all the shit flagged, like they taught you over at City College?"

"Fuck you, man." The kid stomped off, climbed inside his panel van. A small stencil on the passenger door said, Crime Scene Investigations.

Slade shook his head beside me. "I know an ambassador job you could put in for."

"Where's that?"

"Fucking North Korea, Frank. Give the kid a break. You bastard...Are you still drunk?"

"What makes you ask me that? I wasn't drunk in the first place."

"The fuck you weren't."

I shrugged.

"Fuck me," Slade said. "Another body and another fucking midnight."

"That's the gist," I said. "You done set the scene." I shoved my notepad into a shirt pocket. Most cases, I let Slade handle the documentation—he was good at that kind of thing. And, at the time, this case was no different.

"Enrico Frederico Pablo Castaneda. Five-eight, one-ninety-four. Brown hair and eyes. Organ donor." Slade squinted at the Arizona state driver's license in his hand. "Got himself a cartel tattoo on his neck, if I'm not mistaken."

I peered over Slade's shoulder at the small image on the license card. There it was on the guy's skin: Black rosary beads slithering from beneath the collar of his shirt, stretching around behind his neck. I knew the beads led to a depiction of Santa Muerte—Saint Death—over the guy's heart. Cartel? Maybe. Gangbang-er? Likely. Lover? Nope—probably a fighter. "Let's not jump the gun on this one," I said. "Could be he tripped, fell, landed in the damn oil drum."

"Right," Slade said, "And he slammed his fingers in a car door...along with his pecker."

Captain Ryan Jackson, a former Marine with a commendable beer belly and jowls thickening by the month, lifted the crime scene tape for us and we ducked beneath it. "Right this way, boys," he said. "I hope me getting down here before you don't portend a fuckup."

Slade followed close behind Jackson. He said, "I had to pick Frank up is all. Stopped for coffee."

"You two are going to need more than coffee for this one."

I followed with a noncommittal saunter. I liked the captain, but that made me suspicious of him. Like with most of the department, I felt like he was waiting (or hoping) for me to fuck things up for myself. But I cleared cases. Turn enough red into black—hell, they'll let you get away with murder. I hadn't taken it that far yet, but I came close. Most of us did at one time or another. Can't say I'm proud of that, but it's the truth. We followed the captain down a cement path across more dark jetty rocks and smaller riprap. The path split from a cement walkway curved north away from the bridge and ended in a dirt lot next to one of the warehouses. The cement poured into the jetty was not the work of a craftsman. It seemed ill-planned. "What's up with this path, Captain? We know anything about it?"

"Looks like something a few fishermen put in," he said over his shoulder. "Throw a few globs of cement in the right place and you got a staircase to your favorite fishing hole."

The cement steps—they became steps after twenty-five yards or so—descended to the waterline. I could see there was a small stretch of beach there, say fifteen feet wide or so, but it was covered by the tide. The oil drum was sitting in the sand, about one-third covered by lapping water.

And the oil drum was upright.

Slade said, "They put it here. It ain't something that washed up." I nodded along with the captain.

In the oil drum, I saw the lumpy texture of wet hair, one booted foot poking out like a boy's too-loose tooth. I'd have to get closer to see more.

Captain Jackson said, "We got a couple of teenagers found the thing. Boy and a girl. Neon pink fucking hair, if you can believe that. Out here for a little midnight loving. Said they got here and made out for a while, decided to wade in and see what the hell this was. They're high as shit, the two of 'em. Like fucking hot air balloons."

"Nice surprise after a toke or two," I said.

"Yeah, Frank," the captain said, "Must have been a real turn on."

"We'll talk to them tonight." I sneezed twice, wiped my nose with the back of my sleeve. "Before they forget all the important shit."

"We already got them down at the station. Be there until you say they can go home to momma."

Beside us, in a clear storage box marked SDPD, there were a few pairs of wading boots. Slade pulled off his dress shoes, set them in the box one at a time as he slid the boots on over his fancy argyle socks.

"Look at you," I said. "A seasoned pro, down to the toes."

"You look good, you catch more crooks."

"Shit," I said. "Prove that one." I patted my significant beer belly. "The fuck do you think I'm doing?"

He ignored me, stepped into the water and moved toward the oil drum.

Above us, the bottom side of the bridge lifted in pendulum, stretched like a curved cement finger to the first pillar, maybe fifty yards out into the bay. The bridge hit two hundred feet at its apex. It made a hell of a choice for suicides. A sure thing. A majestic and unforgiving sure thing. I knew that as well as anybody in the city, from my beautiful Miranda. I felt my bottom lip start to

16

give as I stared up at the bridge, followed its line to the midpoint. For a moment I imagined what it must have felt like: the wind was cold that night and it would have run through a body like ice. It was a clear night though, a rare night when stars burned through the city's skyline. It must have been like plunging into—

"Frank? You okay, pal?" Slade looked back at me from the water. He had his notepad and pencil out, that determined, hard-ass detective glare on his face. "You alright with this, Frank?"

I cleared my throat, avoided Captain Jackson's eyes. "I'm fine, Skinny. Let's see what we got here on this fine, fucked-up midnight." I removed my shoes and replaced them with wading boots.

Captain Jackson looked uncomfortable, scratched at the folded skin beneath his chin. He coughed once and said, "I'll leave you to it, detectives." He grunted as he climbed upwards along the jetty. Soon, Jackson was gone, vanished over the top of the jagged rocks.

Slade moved toward the oil drum with deliberate caution and observance. I took a deep breath, pushed Miranda from my mind, and stepped into the bay's black and lapping waters.

Chapter 4

In my life, I've seen ugly things.

You don't know evil until you find a dead girl in a suitcase. Or see a single mother gunned down in a liquor store. Or watch a video with masked men beating a teenage kid to a bloody, motionless pulp. I'm not saying this to prove I'm some harbinger of justice—to hell with that. The more I do this job—and the more crimes I solve (or don't solve)—the more I get confused about life, about death, about making bad things right. I know most of what me and Skinny Slade deal with has to do with poverty or drugs. And those two things have to do with money.

Let's call it what it is:

Murder is the street talking back, and the street has a dirty fucking mouth. This was what I was thinking as we sat in our department-issue Ford Focus on a vacant street, a dead man folded into a barrel not more than fifty yards from us.

And missing his fingertips and shriveled dick.

I sipped cold coffee in the passenger seat while Slade checked back over his meticulous notes. Both of us had the bitter taste of vomit on our tongues.

Slade said, "That tech was right about the fingers. Looks like maybe a hand tool. Bolt cutters, I'm betting. Like when you cut through braided cable and have to rip hard to get it to split."

I nodded, looked out at the street and the warehouses. As the night wore on, a gray sheen began to cover everything—part sea mist and part lengthening night. "Maybe, but it's best to let the autopsy do the talking."

"I hear you, Frank. I'm just thinking." Slade turned a page in his notebook, grunted. "Man, hell of a message to cut the guy's Johnson down to a nub."

I finished my coffee, jammed the cup between my legs. "Yeah, it's a fucking sign alright. No doubt, this is some down and dirty drug business. To me, it's weird they left the guy here. Most shit like this goes down in TJ. You and I know that—what's the fucking deal?"

Even sitting here in the car, with the engine running, I could still feel the wet lick of the bay water, the mush of sand beneath my feet. The dead body in the oil drum haunted me: I couldn't shake the look on the vic's face. His eyebrows were flat and black as worms, spread apart over a fat nose. A broad cheek on one side of his face was wedged against his knobby, broken knees. Folded up like a goddamn case file. Cause of death, we thought, might be the small bullet hole just above his heart, in the center of his chest. Not before a shit-ton of torture, though. I figured that, too, would be determined by the autopsy.

"That hole in the vic's chest," Slade said, "probably some small caliber pistol—a put-him-out-of-his-misery shot. You think they got whatever information they wanted?"

Out the windshield, I watched some young patrol officers wander into the street, stand in a circle shooting the shit. Guarding the scene while the techs did their thing. I knew we wouldn't close this case on evidence— we'd close it on word-of-mouth, if we closed it at all. "Maybe the whole thing is a message," I said. "A whodunit for the press. Smoke and mirrors to scare somebody. Another drug kingpin, maybe. Or the feds. A fuck you to CBP, FBI, Border Patrol."

Slade looked up from his notebook, turned his head to squint down the street. Yellow streetlights shined every twenty-five yards or so, breaking the night gray like weary spotlights on a community theater stage. "You see a reporter somewhere? A fucking news van?"

I shook my head. "Not yet, Skinny. Not until you get on the horn." Slade, like I said before, was a ladies' man. He had romantic notions when it came to a few local news reporters. The man knew what it was to diversify—he had print, TV, and radio in his portfolio.

Slade grinned, looked back to his notes. "You know I'm exclusive with Georgia now."

"Georgia Frost, from the UT?" A beautiful lady—if a little tomboy-like—who worked the crime beat on weekends. She taught elementary school during the weekdays. It's hard in San Diego for journalists. "Miss wannabe Edna Buchanan?"

"You got it, Frank. Exclusive as a downtown club, baby."

"How long has it just been Georgia?"

"Week or two." Slade flipped another page in his notebook.

"Shit," I said. "A week ain't time, man. It's a breath. A blink of an eye. If that. Talk to me when you got twenty-five years in the thing." I leaned down and peered out my window at the scythe-shaped bridge. I wanted to think Miranda didn't feel pain, that she died without any hurt. But I knew that wasn't true. It couldn't be true. "Talk to me," I said, "when you get the wind knocked out of you by the lady with one goddamn look. She can do that to you, you got time into it. Good time, too. Over-fucking-time."

"No, Frank," Slade said. He was looking at me, the bottoms of his eyes shiny and wet. "I ain't got any time into it. Not a damn second worth counting." He frowned and tried to clear his throat. Must have had a frog in there. He said, "I sure miss your wife, Frank."

"Me too. Goddamn. I miss her too." We sat there in silence. The street cops kept telling dirty jokes and the night stood as still as a dead man's promise. The gray had given way to black and I wanted the morning to come before I got too deep into the cold blackness of my own depression.

Yeah, I thought, I've seen some ugly things in my life.

Sure have run into some beauty, though. Plenty of beauty out here in the devil's playground. But that's a twisted hell, too. Because every second somebody's got to die.

And one night it was my wife, Miranda.

One night it was Miranda.

Fucking bridges.

I sighed and said, "We better get our asses back to the station, talk to those teenage lovebirds."

Chapter 5

I don't understand pink hair.

But who does?

When I sat down across from Celeste Richards—five-four and one-ten, seventeen years old—she looked at me like I was fuzz, like she knew the back seat of a patrol car better than the inside of her own head. She nodded at the interrogation room's beige, graffiti-covered walls. "You should hire a new decorator—this place makes me feel like slitting my wrists." Her mouth turned down in dramatic disgust.

I smacked my lips, opened my notebook to a blank page. I stared at the tip of my pencil before pinning her with a cop's glare. Sometimes, with kids, it worked.

Celeste shrugged, ran purple fingernails through her pink hair. "Can I go now? My mom's going to be pissed if she wakes up for work and sees I'm gone."

"What's mom do?" I sucked coffee grounds from between my teeth, ran my tongue across my lower lip.

"Dudes like you."

"Really? Your mom works the street? What's her name?"

The teenage girl's face softened—she was afraid of me,

or she loved her mom. I saw her regret the implication that her mom was a hooker. There was a human inside Celeste somewhere, despite her teenage exterior. "My mom's a nurse at Mercy Hospital." She looked down at the fold-away table, ran one index finger in an oval pattern across the table's surface. Without looking at me, she said, "You don't have to tell her about this, do you?"

"So you're a fake tough kid. The whole punk facade, is that it?"

"I'm a fucking teenager, old man." She looked at me and I noticed her eyes were hazel. Same color as my wife's. And my daughter's. Celeste tugged at a lock of pink hair. "This is just to piss my mom off."

I smiled. "Bet it worked. How's it going to be when I drop you off this morning?"

"C'mon, sir. I can get home on my own. Don't tell my mom about this. She'll fucking—"

"What are you going to give me, Celeste?"

"About that?"

"What were you and..." I consulted a page in my notebook. "Turner, sweet little Turner, doing under the bridge tonight?"

Celeste's face got pissy again. Her eyebrows crunched down on her button nose and she twisted her mouth toward one cheek. "I was giving him a blow job. What do you think?"

"Midnight romance, huh?"

"Fuck you, man."

"Your momma teach you to talk to cops like that?"

Celeste sighed. "It's our two-month anniversary, okay? We just wanted to make out and smoke some weed. That's all it was. It's a place to be alone... together."

"You go down there a lot?"

"Not really."

"What time did you leave your house with Turner?"

Celeste looked at a pink Hello Kitty watch on her left wrist. "He came over at eight. When my mom fell asleep we snuck out. I think we left at, maybe, ten-ish? I don't know, man. Am I going to get my phone back soon?"

"And it takes how long to get to the bay bridge from your house?"

"Turner's friend dropped us off. It took, like, ten minutes or something."

"What's the friend's name?"

Celeste leaned back in the chair, crossed her arms. "Ask Turner. It's his friend."

"I'm asking you, Celeste." I straightened in my chair. Nothing like a teenage girl to try your patience. I thought about my daughter, Kimmie. She was twenty-eight, worked as a barista in Oakland. Fucking liberal arts education. As a teen, Kimmie liked to push buttons. She'd ask you to pick her up and get a ride with a friend instead. Told us she was a lesbian during the summer before her senior year. Then went to senior prom with the second-string quarterback. Truth was, I didn't know much about Kimmie, the adult version of her.

I felt a glob of deep shame form and solidify in my belly.

The last time I saw Kimmie was at Miranda's funeral. A new tattoo peeked out the top of her black blouse, creeped along the too-visible fold of her cleavage. We stood over Miranda's grave, just the two of us. Kimmie's younger brother couldn't make it—something about a court date for a corporate client. Goddamn lawyers. Always too fucking busy to see off the dead. I

24

supposed that's why we have preachers. Still, I was pissed at Norton. And I was too grief-stricken to comfort Kimmie. Or too chicken-shit. She cried like a toddler and I stood there with my dark sunglasses on, big fat tears hiding behind my eyeballs. Yeah, chicken-shit. That was it.

I thought I better call Kimmie. Though I doubted she would answer.

Celeste sighed from her toes and said, "I think his name is, like, Rambo or something. Can I go home now? Can I have my fucking cell phone back?" She shifted in her chair, pinched the bridge of her nose between pinkie finger and thumb. "You're killing my high, you know that?"

"Rambo, like the Stallone movie?"

Celeste said, "Who's that?"

Jesus. I found it hard to believe Sylvester Stallone's pure and absolute genius could be lost on anybody, teenage girls included. "You don't know Sly Stallone? What are you, some kind of loser?" I listed the greats, ticked them off on my fingers one by one. "First Blood. Rocky. Rocky II, III. Shit, all the Rocky flicks. Cop Land. That Get Carter remake."

"It's like you're speaking a different language." Celeste shook her head, bent her lips into a pout.

"Okay, wait. How about The Expendables?"

"Oh, that's one of those stupid action movies, right?"

Stupid action movie? Wow, I thought, these fucking kids need a lesson in—

The door swung open behind me and Slade's voice came, "Frank—I need you to get in here for a second."

I stood and shook my finger at Celeste. "We're going to finish this, Celeste. I'll be back."

"Whatever. Bring my fucking phone, okay?"

I could feel Celeste's glare as I followed Slade out the door and down the hall.

Turner Malcolm, unlike his girlfriend, did have a bit of street inside him. He was a burly nineteen-year-old with a long scar running across his forehead. His short hair, like Celeste's, was colored pink. He had mean little eyes set back in deep sockets. He wore the garb of a high school goth kid: black Doc Marten boots, tight black jeans, and a black T-shirt with a heavy metal band on the front—The Liars. Turner leaned backwards in his seat when we walked in, belched with punkish bragga-docio. "One fat cop and one skinny cop," he said. "Tweedle-Dee and Tweedle-Dum. Sweet. It's like an after school special or something."

Me and Slade took our seats.

"Let's get back to your friend," Slade said. His note-book, now flat on the table, was full with scribbled notes. "Frank here wants to listen, too. If you don't mind."

"Whatever, man."

Slade said, "So, this Rambo guy, he told you—"

"He knows where a couple bodies are buried."

"And when did he say this?" I thought Turner knew how to lie. It's a craft you learn in group homes and squatter flats from the Mexican border all the way on up to Canada. His eyes kept their color and shape when he spoke, but his forehead scar wrinkled slightly above his nose.

"Before he dropped us off tonight. Well, last night."

"In the car?" I put both elbows on the fold-away

table and cupped my hands over my mouth.

"Yeah, in the car."

"You know," I said, "putting a couple bodies on somebody is no joke—we're murder police, buddy. You give us some jive about bodies and we got to go figure out what's what."

Turner shrugged.

"Okay," Slade said, "what exactly did your buddy Rambo tell you?"

Turner crossed one booted foot over his knees, rested his hands on the leather boot. "We're driving down University and he starts talking about some guy he knows." Turner snapped his fingers. "Guy named Riddick. This guy does contract work for one of those Mexican cartels. Except Rambo said they aren't Mexican because they're American. Citizens, you know? I mean, I guess they work for the cartel or something. It's like a company."

"Riddick what?" Slade kept his pen moving this whole time. "Give me the last name."

"Didn't say."

"Figures," I said.

Turner rolled his eyes. "Anyway, I guess Riddick had to do a whole family for these cartel people. Some corporate guy who pissed the fuckers off. A, uh, what is it...guy who owns car dealerships or whatever."

I looked at Slade—his brown peepers were already pinned to my face: The Jacoby family.

Mark Jacoby, his wife, and their fourteen-year-old daughter had been missing for about six months. Disappeared without telling family, friends, or business associates. This scandal ran across the papers for a week or two. It was a federal investigation with SDPD involved as support. Took the case from my pal Donovan and his partner, an ex-college football player named Richie. There was evidence the family had been abducted, trafficked over state lines into Nevada. The Missing Persons Unit was all too happy to get rid of what looked like an unsolvable case. I wrote a note to myself:

Run by Richie or Donovan's desk—ask about Feds.

Slade put his eyes back on Turner. "And what did Rambo tell you about the bodies?"

"He said they were out near Jacumba, east county." Turner said the name with a hard J, like us white people always say it. "Some BLM land where nobody thinks to look. The cartel dumps people out there sometimes."

Now this, to me, sounded like street talk, a queer manifestation of the American Tall Tale. Throw one punch and say you landed a thousand. Let the legend do its work. I said, "You're full of shit, Turner."

"Whatever, fat man. Suit yourself. Don't believe me if you don't want to."

"Why tell us now?" Slade asked.

"You're asking me about this other thing, the dead guy in the oil thingy, and I figured this shit might be info you want. Rambo told me this shit, like, six hours ago."

Again, me and Slade met gazes. I lifted my chin and tilted my head—let's go outside for a second. We told Turner to wait and stepped into the hall. Slade stared at his notebook, pinched a leaf of lined paper between thumb and index finger. I leaned back against the wall, closed my eyes. I knew we wouldn't get much sleep over the next few days. You got a short window of time when it comes to a homicide. Urban legend and statistics say it's forty-eight hours, but we knew better—it's a whole lot less than that. Part of why me and Slade were so good had to do with our willingness to work without sleep. For me, mezcal helped. For Slade, it was Red Bull and thick black coffee.

Slade said, "You want to run by and talk to Richie or Donovan, ask them about the feds?"

"Yeah, I'll call as soon as it's light outside, if they aren't around."

"We need to corroborate this with the girl."

"I'll go in there now. Trust me, she's about ready to go home. She'll give it up."

Slade nodded.

"He say much about the guy in the oil drum?" I felt like, somehow, we'd gotten too far away from our own cold body.

"Yeah, man. He said they were making out and the girl saw something in the water. Said he hoped it was a bale of Mary Jane or something."

"Like how they wash up on the beach every now and then?"

"That's right. Fucking kids, man. Said he got out there and almost shit his pants. That's when they called it in."

"It's weird though," I said. "This guy Rambo runs his mouth and then they end up seeing another body, and maybe it's cartel work."

"You thinking Rambo wanted the body found? That maybe he dumped it there?" Slade's eyebrows dipped into a capital V. The man even looked like he could think his way out of a ten-thousand-piece puzzle.

"But to do that," I said, "Rambo's got to know Turner will ask for a ride, and he's got to know where the lovebirds will want to go."

"Maybe they aren't lovebirds," Slade said. "Maybe

that's all bullshit?"

"You're saying it's their job to give us the body?"

Slade said, "Could be."

"That just doesn't make sense."

At that moment, Slade's cell phone rang and he answered. "Yeah, this is Ryerson." He listened for a few seconds and said, "I appreciate it." He hung up and nodded at me. "Well, the Johnson in the jar belongs, it seems, to Enrico Frederico."

I thought for a while and finally said, "You think they'll sew that thing back on? Before they put him in the dirt, I mean?"

Slade pondered that, but didn't answer.

I said, "Let me drive the girl home, see if I can get some answers from her."

"Do that," Slade said. "I'll keep fucking around with numb-nuts Turner."

Chapter 6

No sun yet over the city.

Gray light outlining the streets and buildings. Above us, one of the first incoming flights of the day roared toward the airport, full with pale-skinned tourists and wacky-headed business people. My buzz long gone, I had no trouble steering the Ford onto the freeway, getting up to speed. Celeste sat in the passenger seat with her arms crossed, a smug teenager look on her face. "What exit, Celeste?"

"It's faster if you get off on Washington, head east."

"Fancy-smancy," I said. "I thought your momma was a nurse."

"My daddy," she said with sarcasm, "is an asshole lawyer. We haven't seen him in six months."

"Is that what hanging out with Turner is for, to deal with your absent daddy complex?"

She chuckled. "You think you're so smart."

"No," I said. "I'm of average intelligence. And that's all it takes to see you're fucking things up. One day, you keep going like this, you're going to wake up in a dingy apartment, common law married to a guy named Spike, has a head tattoo and filed down teeth. You won't have a career, not unless you call working girl a valid choice. You'll be thirty years old with saggy tits and an ass that keeps getting bigger. Best you'll hope for is a John with a little generosity and—"

"Okay, old man," Celeste said. "I fucking get it. Turner's a loser. You think I don't know that?"

I took the Washington exit, turned right without braking, and headed up the curved road toward the uptown area. We passed a restaurant called Sapphire's. I took my wife there for our last anniversary—twenty-five years of marriage. Two decades and some change. More time than a dictator in an African police state. Shit, longer than most folks have a career. Twenty-five years on PD and I could bail out if I wanted, take my decent pension. I was one year away from that, and from the big five-oh. Fifty. But now my wife was gone. Not a damn thing to live for.

Miranda wore a purple dress that night. It hung loose across her shoulders and tapered tight over her hips. I remembered how it cupped the shape of her breasts and ended just above her knees. She never used much jewelry, but that night she had on diamond earrings I bought her years before—Christmas present, I think— and a dainty silver bracelet on her left wrist. Auburn hair to just below her neckline. A beautiful woman escorted by a fat cop with too many open murder cases. What can I say, sometimes a man gets lucky. And that was me. What did we talk about that night? Our kids. Retirement. The next two-week trip to the Yucatán. And all that, to her, must not have meant fuck all. Because Miranda jumped from that bridge.

Dead the instant she hit water.

I put my mind back on the Castaneda case, back on

this Rambo guy who was supposedly talking about dead bodies. We hit a village area with more restaurants, a grocery store, pubs and coffee shops.

"Take a left here," Celeste said.

I made the turn and she told me to stop near a nice-looking mid-century-style house. Floor-to-ceiling windows and metalwork for accent. "Nice place. Daddy must be a fancy lawyer, huh?"

"Criminal defense," Celeste said. "The best kind. What were you thinking about just now?"

I looked over at the pink-haired punk teenager and saw, in her eyes, a caring I hadn't felt in months. Not beyond the ceaseless worry of Skinny Slade, at least—god bless the man. I said, "I'm just thinking about a dead family buried somewhere out near Jacumba." The name came out right, like the J was a Y. "I hear there's a fourteen-year-old girl dead. Buried. In an unmarked—"

"I thought he was fucking with Turner, trying to scare me." She looked away, squinted in anger at her father's empty house.

"Rambo?"

"Yeah," she said. "That's his nickname. I don't know his real name. You're saying he wasn't just talking."

"I'm saying it sounds, maybe, like it could be true. You remember the name he mentioned?"

Celeste said, "Jacoby. It was Jacoby. He said, 'Those dumb ass Jacobys got killed and we buried them out near Jacumba.' Like it was, I don't know, clobbering a mailbox with a baseball bat. He was acting like it was supposed to be funny." She sighed and looked back to me, this time with hurt in her eyes.

"It sure as shit isn't funny. Might be a true fact. He say anything more definite about location?"

Celeste furrowed her brow. "I think he might have said near the border, near the border fence. But, I mean, the fence is, like, super-long or whatever."

Okay, I thought. That's something. "You going to tell me what you two were doing down there tonight?" I watched her without blinking. Pretty girl. If you took away the pink hair.

"It was Turner and Rambo—they just said it was private." She hesitated. Her lips worked for a minute before her voice came out: "I'm a virgin and...I really was going to give him a blow job. Am I that fucking stupid? It didn't happen, but am I that fucking stupid?"

I thought about my beautiful wife plummeting head-first toward the bay's cold black water, hard as cement when you fall from that height. Or when you jump. Or when you're pushed. "Listen, sister," I said. "A blow job ain't a big mistake. It's just bad judgment. You can come back from a blow job. Some things, though..."

"Like being dead?"

"Right, like murder. You don't come back from that."

Celeste sighed again. Her voice jumped in her throat. She waited half a minute before saying, "I think Turner knows something about the dead guy. I don't know why. I just...do."

I nodded and said, "Thanks for coming clean with me—I appreciate it. Now, get inside before mom notices you're gone." I handed her my business card and pointed at the cell number. "Give me a call if you think of anything else. Or, if you hear anything from Turner."

"You're not going to talk to my mom?"

I laughed. "Sister, you ain't under arrest. Didn't your daddy teach you anything?"

Chapter 7

Thirty minutes after I dropped Celeste, I met Slade at a dive bar near my place. Open and serving drinks at six in the morning. Big surprise it was us two and the bartender. Slade ordered instant coffee. I got a tumbler full of bourbon without asking. "Thanks, Randy. Appreciate it," I said.

The old bartender ambled down the bar, leaned over a real-life city newspaper—he studied the sports page with religious intensity.

Slade told me he cut Turner loose with a tail—newbie detective we called QB, short for quarterback. I forgot his real name, but he—like Slade—had himself a fancy degree or two. I was suspicious of cops with law degrees because it marked you in a different class, from what I could tell. I still remember the years my son studied for his JD—I swear it was like watching a slow-motion transition to absolute asshole. The kid wore tailored suits now, and he drank expensive red wine. In other words, I felt like he was somebody else's kid. That's what a law degree does to you. And to your family.

"You think QB will lose the kid?"

Slade shrugged. "God knows I don't want to follow

the punk. I know you don't either. QB wants the OT—man's wife is with child." He rubbed one side of his face. His five o'clock shadow sounded like sandpaper on cement. "You talk to Kimmie or Norton lately?"

I finished my drink, tapped the glass on the bar. Randy grunted, left his newspaper and poured me another. "What's that got to do with this fucking case?" It came out more angry than it felt.

"Jesus, Slim Fat. I'm just asking. Because the...Well, because I mentioned the kid." Slade slumped on his bar stool, shook his head.

Nothing like a cop being pissed at his partner to hold up a murder case. "It's fine. I know you didn't mean anything by it." We sat in silence for some time, thinking about dead bodies and lopped off weeners. "I been meaning to call Kimmie. Seeing this girl tonight reminded me that, shit, I don't even know my own fucking daughter. You believe that? It's damn odd, the way people change."

Slade slurped coffee. The thing about Slade—and this helped him as a cop—was that he knew when to shut up, when to let things be.

I said, "That bridge, standing under it, looking up, that got to me a little. I keep wondering why she did it, you know? And it wouldn't matter if it was a small reason, something simple. Just any meaning behind it would help." I sighed and drank more bourbon. "Ain't death a bitch?"

Slade nodded.

The bar's front door opened and a wino stumbled in. He wore dirty Levi's and flip-flops, a flannel shirt over bark-colored skin.

Randy stood and crossed his arms. "I told you you're

eighty-sixed, Freddo."

"The hell with that. I been drinking here since before you—"

"Get the fuck out." Randy stood taller behind the bar. It was like the man grew when he got angry. I wondered if the same thing happened with me. I'd seen it in Skinny Slade, and some other cops I knew. Not all of them were straight either. I'd learned that rage, given the right direction, could be a force for good. It could be the opposite of that, too.

Slade swiveled toward the wino and cleared his throat. He pulled open his coat at the collar, revealed the badge hanging from a chain around his neck, like it was some goddamn ancient talisman. Fucking movie star cops.

The wino hacked a loogie onto the carpet, backed away, exited the bar. Randy nodded at us, went back to reading the box scores.

Slade said, "You get anything from Celeste?"

"She said that Rambo kid mentioned the border fence. But, like she said, that doesn't nail things down necessarily. Both of them mentioned Jacumba though. That sounds like it's worth a look. Maybe we head out there today, ask around a bit."

"After we talk to Rambo."

"Shit," I said. "You know where to look?"

"Apartment complex in Mid-City. Rent-controlled. You know the kind of place."

"What are we waiting for then? Let's hit him while he's passed out."

Slade nodded and scratched his chin. "After I get some more coffee. You know what, I went out to Jacumba a couple months ago with..." He paused. "A lady friend, let's say. Horseback riding. Sweat my damn ass off out there."

"Wait a second," I said. "You're telling me you, Skinny Slade Ryerson, went horseback riding?"

"Cowboy up, motherfucker."

"I'd have paid to see that." It was my turn to shake my head. I couldn't see this pretty boy chasing after some news anchor on horseback. It was an image too far from reality.

"Twenty bucks and I'll show you a picture."

"You let her snap a pic of you?"

Slade said, "It's for my scrapbook."

"Shit."

"Twenty bucks and I'll let you see it. Point to this, though, is something I noticed. There's a fence out there on the border, like most other places. But I noticed there's a big part on each side where there's no fence. It's just rocky hills and—"

"You're saying the fence—the border fence—doesn't have fence on each side. Like, it's not a fence? Because, if you ask me, a fence unfinished ain't really a fence."

"What I'm saying is the fence runs up against rough terrain. There's no way to put a fence along—"

"The hell there isn't. A fence is a fucking fence."

Slade finished his coffee, smacked his lips and sighed. "Again, point is, there's a distinct stretch of border fence."

"And maybe that's what Rambo was talking about," I said. "Could be."

"Yes, it could."

Slade said, "I say we go find out."

We stood and dropped a crumpled ten on the bar. Randy nodded. As we walked out, he said, "A fence is a fence, boys. Where it stops, that's where it ain't a fence no more. Doesn't take a detective to see that, does it?"

We waved over our shoulders. I guessed Randy should have been a big thinker in some kind of government institute. It's too bad where some people end up in this life.

Chapter 8

We parked in the alley behind Rambo's building, a three-story apartment complex with graffiti running along the back wall. I saw, too, the windows had wrought-iron cages over them. Rambo lived in a shitty section of the city—city council kept saying it was "next on the list" for earmarked tax revenue, but the voter turnout said dick to politicians, even the scummy local kind. Slade did narcotics work in the neighborhood when he first joined the department. I knew the city well—hell, it was the place of my birth—but I let Slade take the lead around here.

Ahead, in the early morning gloom, a gray-black cat crossed through the alley, jumped into a trash dumpster. "Breakfast for miss kitty," I said.

Slade chuckled. "We all eat shit sometimes."

"Or all the time," I said.

Slade shut off the car and we watched for a few minutes. Out one window, a thin trail of smoke drifted through the screen, threaded upward over the building's roof. It was the only window without a cage covering it. Odd, but I thought little about it. Slade pointed and said, "Address is 5C, and that might be third floor back.

That might be our boy right there."

"Could be."

"What do you think about one of us hanging back here?"

I didn't like that. Best to stay together in the hood, cops or not. "How about we call patrol, let a cruiser hang out here and wait?"

Slade called it in and we waited.

About ten minutes later a black and white cruiser slid down the alley opposite our car. I put my hand out the window, signaled for the patrol cop to stay back from the building, not tip Rambo or some other scumbag with a warrant. Place like this, you roll up on two or three ex-cons and they all start running. They do that and we're obligated to chase. God knew, I wasn't in shape for that.

"Let's go," Slade slid from the car like a real TV cop, all sly smile and liquid walk. I followed behind him, grunting and laboring with the slight bourbon buzz and a sleepless night.

We circled onto the main street, turned right after passing a rundown liquor store, and went up three flights of outdoor stairs. Slade waited for me at the top, raised his eyebrows in judgment. "We need to get you back to the slim part of slim fat. You need to hit the gym, Frank."

"That, or I could stop drinking so much."

My partner shrugged and moved down the open-air corridor past a few doorways. Images of the Virgin de Guadalupe stared back at us from windows and doors. I heard a Mexican tenor singing malaise in one apartment and the sound of children—even this early in the morning—was like a hum that wouldn't quit.

Slade slowed as he reached 5C. The front window was covered with a child's sheet—Teenage Mutant Ninja Turtles—and Slade squinted through it to see inside the room. "I can't see shit, Frank. Can you?"

I squinted too and saw nothing. On the door, I noticed a small postcard with an image of Santa Muerte taped over the peephole. There it was again, that image of Saint Death. "Just knock on the door and get this shit over with. I doubt the kid's a sicario. Shit, he's probably just repeating something he heard on the corner, or from somebody down at the disco."

Slade drew his sidearm and I guffawed.

He said, "Shit, Frank. Get out your fucking gun."

"This early in the morning?"

"Man, you want to get shot in the hood on a Thursday?"

"You know these motherfuckers can't aim worth shit. Fat chance he—"

"The fuck you fuzz want, man!"

Both me and Slade looked at the door. Slade moved back into the corridor.

I said, "That you, Rambo? We need to ask you some things about your pal. Kid named Turner."

"What's Turner into?"

I pounded on the door with my fist. "Let us in, Rambo. We just have some questions."

A door farther back in the corridor opened and an old Latina woman poked her head out to look at us. A knowing gaze crossed her face—la policia again, it said. Siempre.

Slade waved her back inside and her door closed with the audible clunk of a dead bolt.

"What the fuck you want with me?"

The voice sounded farther from the door, huddled up somewhere back in the apartment.

Slade said, "It's just for background info, Rambo. You ain't in trouble, man—I fucking promise."

"Two cops at my door and I ain't in trouble."

I shook my head, thought maybe Rambo was smarter than we knew. I looked at Slade and he waved his sidearm at me. Jesus, I thought, it's too early in the day for this shit. I unholstered my own gun, a 9 mm. "It's the police, Rambo. Open up or we're coming in. Don't make me break down this door, man." Not legal, but worth a try.

Rambo didn't answer. As I was about to pound on the door again, we heard the cop out back chirp his cruiser's siren. And then we heard the unmistakable sound of a V-8 engine accelerating through the alley and out into the main street.

"Right or left, Frank? Speak up, dammit!"

"Left here! Watch out, man!"

Slade slammed on the brakes as we entered an intersection, almost smacking a middle-aged junk collector on a bicycle. He flipped us the bird and kept weaving across the street, both lanes empty in the early morning. Except for two detectives in a department-issue Ford Focus, a black and white police cruiser, and a crook named Rambo on foot. Evidently, working as a crook paid dividends for cardio fitness. The man was a wizard on his feet. After we heard the cruiser take off, Slade and me hustled down the apartment building stairs, came around the corner, and saw Rambo sprinting like an Olympian across the street, the cruiser close behind.

Rambo leaped over a chain-link fence between a shoe repair store and a piñata shop, disappeared down a long alley. The cruiser made the next left while Slade ran for the car. I waited on the street to see if Rambo would double back—it didn't happen.

Next thing I knew, Slade squealed to a stop next to me and I hopped into the car. Now, we were circling the block, Slade pumping the gas and yelling at me.

"I'm going right at the next alley," Slade said.

The car's engine whined like a two-stroke motorcycle. I ran a hand along my seat belt to make sure it was tight. While I did that, I caught a flash of white through Slade's window—a hooded sweatshirt. "Left! Left! I saw the fucker!"

Slade mashed the brakes again and yanked the wheel. We spun counter-clockwise, left rubber on the black pavement, and Slade steered the car down the alley. As the stucco walls closed in on us, I saw the white flash from behind a trash dumpster—it had to be him: Rambo sprinted into the center of the alley. He put his head down and pumped.

Slade said, "The fucker is fast."

"You got that right."

"Let me put you up next to him."

"Go, go-go-go-go!"

An opening revealed itself in the alley—two side streets—and Slade punched it. I saw Rambo's surprised expression as we passed on his left. My seat belt slapped against the door as I unbuckled it. I opened my door, Slade slowed and, at that instant, I lunged from the car and hit Rambo square in the chest. I'm a heavy man and Rambo's breath left him like an explosion. I felt the mushroom cloud in my face. We hit the hard pavement, skidded, and rolled twice before I straddled him across the back side and yanked his right arm back over his hip. I applied pressure.

Rambo screamed, "My fucking arm, fuzz. Don't break it!"

"I'll rip it off if you don't stop fighting." I pulled up and out at Rambo's elbow.

He squealed.

"Frank, let him be. Frank. Frank." It was Slade pulling at my collar, telling me to let up on the runner. "Easy, Frank. Let's not fuck up the paperwork on this thing."

I cuffed Rambo and Slade helped me bring him to his feet. Seconds later, the patrol officer arrived. The engine beneath his cruiser's hood ticked and hummed. We waved the patrol cop off and he pumped the siren again and sped off to chase some other brown, black, or poor man. I threw Rambo against the car, placed my hands on my hips, and stared him dead in the face. "Why the fuck you run from us, motherfucker?"

"Because, man. You gonna do me wrong."

"The fuck you mean, 'do you wrong'?" Slade frisked Rambo and spat another phrase at him. "You do your-fucking-self wrong being a loser and a junkie, man. You don't need no help to get got." Slade backed away, waited for the rage that was sure to erupt.

"I almost got away."

"Shit," I said. "We were just about to call in the ghetto bird, spotlight your ass."

Slade grunted. "We don't need a chopper to find this fucker. He'd probably go home for a peanut butter sandwich."

"Yo, man. Let me go. I'm begging you."

I laughed a big, hearty laugh like I hadn't done in a few months. Or not that I remembered.

"I ain't kidding, man. I'm begging—you got to let me go." Rambo's eyes shot around at the buildings on the street. "Before they see, man. This shit gonna get me got, for real."

"Before who sees?" Slade knew lies as well as he knew women.

"Fucking eyes in the sky, man. Eyes in the sky."

"What are you," I said, "another nutso?"

Rambo's eyes started to get shiny. Within seconds, he wept. He fell to his knees and his shoulders bobbed with grief. Wails seeped from his throat. He choked out a few phrases. "It's already done, man. You already got me killed. Shit don't matter now."

I kneeled down beside Rambo, lifted his peach-fuzzed chin with my index finger. "Who you talking about, Rambo?" I looked up at the sky, back to the kid's wet eyes. "Who's watching?"

He looked me square in the face and said, "The king of the streets, man. Fucking God almighty his damn self."

"You religious, Rambo?"

"No, man. I ain't talking about no church god. I'm talking about the real fucking thing."

I stared at the weeping thug and thought about my dead wife, her tiny pale body buried six feet deep in Forest Lawn. "Real god, huh?" I said it with bitterness on my lips.

"The cartel, man—fucking demons."

We tried to get Rambo to tell us more, but he kept insisting he was dead, that he didn't exist. And if the man thought he was dead, on the real, how the hell could we argue with that?

Chapter 9

We thought about taking Rambo in, booking him for some bullshit thing. But it wouldn't get us anything besides paperwork. We let him go. About two hours later, while Slade did research on the dead man—Castaneda—I called a sheriff's deputy I knew who worked out near Jacumba. Man I used to meet for drinks when he came to the city.

I stared at a half-eaten egg burrito on my desk and listened to Lengo's cell phone ring and go to voicemail: "This is Lengo. I'm at work. Use your words and I'll call you back."

"Lengo, it's Frank. Caught a body today—well, yesterday—and I'm hearing rumors about Jacumba. The Jacoby family thing came up. Thought I'd loop you in. Call me back."

I hung up and took another big bite from my breakfast burrito. Scrambled eggs, bacon, potatoes, and red salsa. Nothing like it, but my stomach turned as I chewed and swallowed. Murder always did that to me, upset my stomach.

I told myself: The day a murder doesn't make me sick is the day I'm done as a detective. And as a human.

Across the room, in another cubicle, I heard Slade speaking Spanglish, jawing gangster-like about strip clubs in Tijuana. Tapping his CI network, I supposed. That meant Castaneda didn't hit in the system—no criminal record. If it was true, I'd shit myself with surprise.

But I'd seen weirder shit. Working as a cop on the border, you got to see—

My cell phone buzzed. I put down my burrito and answered the call. "Lengo, que paso, amigo? You up early, or you just get home?"

"Late night, Frank," Lengo said. "And a long morning. A tractor-trailer flipped on the eastbound highway. Had to be a fuel tanker, of course. We called haz mat, stood around for six hours. You know how it is. What's all this about the Jacoby family?"

"Me and Skinny caught a body late last night. Kind of a sick scene, buddy." I detailed the murder and Castaneda's mutilation, caught Lengo up on Rambo's story (taken secondhand from the punk teen, Turner). "What I was wondering, you got anybody with Border Patrol I can call unofficial-like? Hate to make hay over some kid's loudmouth lie, but I also want to check out that area, make sure the kid really is lying, you know?"

Lengo said, "You want to confirm the lie you suspect."

"That's right."

"Be a whole lot easier if motherfuckers just...Told the pinche truth."

"I'm with you, Lengo." I picked up my burrito with one hand, shoved the rest of it into my mouth. I tried to chew in silence, but it didn't work.

"The fuck are you eating, Frank?"

I finished chewing, swallowed. "Burrito," I said, rolling my tongue like a cartoon character.

"Sounds like you're real invested in this murder, Frank."

"Man's got to eat. You're no good if you don't eat."

"I know a BP guy who rides the fence line, but he's just your run-of-the-mill agent."

"Doesn't have to be J. Edgar Hoover. Just want to get the lay of the land out there."

Lengo gave me the agent's personal number and said, "If you two dicks get out here, send me a text. We'll meet for a beer and some wings. Anything comes up on the Jacoby missing persons case, I need to know. My boss will give me bullshit if I'm not keyed in with the feds. The dude hates G-men. I think it's because he's corrupt."

"I'll let you know, Lengo. Thanks for the contact, hermano." We hung up and I dialed the number Lengo provided. The line rang for a while and, as I was about to hang up, Border Patrol agent Hector Candida answered.

"This Hector, what up?"

"Agent Candida? This is detective Frank Pinson, SDPD. Buddy of mine gave me your number and I wanted to talk—"

"Who?" He cut me off without consideration.

I said, "Deputy Lengo over at—"

"Don't know him, buddy."

"I'm sure you do," I said. "I just talked to him about—"

"I ain't no Border Patrol no more."

"Well, you live out near Jacumba? I wanted to—"

"I don't know you, buddy." His voice got gruff,

condescending. "I ain't working at that job no more and I live out in Calexico. I got nothing for you—"

"I'm murder police, Candida. I don't give two fucks if you don't work that job no more. I want some fucking questions answered, and you're going to answer them."

Candida laughed. "Homicide, huh? Who got put down?"

The way he said it, "put down," set my gut moving—tiny details like that said one of two things to a detective: This guy is either bad news or he wants to pretend he's bad news. Candida? Bad news. I wondered for a moment why Lengo passed along this one's name. Maybe he did it on purpose. That, of all things, wouldn't surprise me. Lengo was a longtime deputy, and he found himself—after eighteen years of service—fed up with corruption and bureaucracy and hypocritical bullshit. Give me something without giving me anything—I saw Lengo doing that. Why not? I put my thoughts back on Candida. "You want to know who? I don't know, amigo. You got any friends missing?"

Candida said, "Friends, no. Enemies missing? Could be."

"Okay, smart ass."

"A detective without humor…What are you, married?"

I said, "Used to be."

"So, that's it then."

"What is?"

He said, "Your bad attitude."

"Dude, you're the one with the attitude. I'm just calling about a thing happened a few months back." I paused and sneezed. "When did you get out of the job?"

He scoffed over the line. "Two months ago."

"Why?"

"None of your fucking business."

I said, "You remember the Jacoby family missing persons case?" The case was high enough profile that all agencies were alerted at one time or another.

"What about it?"

"Ran into a CI who said something about they're buried—the family that is—out near Jacumba."

Candida did not speak. Heavy breathing started on the line.

"You ever hear anything about that, or about bodies out in the desert? Maybe from the migrants you picked up, or people you met?"

I looked up to see Slade standing over me. He tapped one side of his head—he had something for us about Castaneda.

"One sec, Skinny," I said and turned my attention back to the phone. But the line was silent and, a second or two later, it was all dial tone. Hector Candida, former Border Patrol agent, hung up on me.

Chapter 10

"What it is," Slade said, "is a damn mystery how this dude Castaneda got got."

"And why's that?" We crossed the street swiveling our heads to dodge traffic. The shadow of the court-house shaded the entire block. We reached the sidewalk and took the few steps into the county's laudable seat of popular justice. Slade wanted coffee, and I needed it. We nodded at the sheriff's deputies manning the metal detector, slid through and walked into the jury lounge, firearms still on our hips. "Man looked like a gangbang-er," I said. "It ain't a mystery he got murdered. It's a mystery who did it. Or maybe, who the hell didn't do it."

Slade walked this whole way with both hands plunged into the pockets of his flat-front slacks. He looked confused, or worried. We both poured coffee from the pot at the back of the jury lounge. By this time in the morning—eight o' the clock—grumpy jurors were filing in, taking seats in the conference-style room. We ambled through the crowd, pushed our way through the incoming line, and walked out onto the sidewalk. We stood there and stared at the passing throng of homeless, young professionals, line cooks, tourists.

Slade sipped his coffee, made a deep-creased face. "I got a CI, Frank..." He shook his head. "This CI says Castaneda, dick-less himself, was a cartel enforcer. A fucking rager, Frank. I'm saying he's a bad dude, and he's done some evil shit. Killings. Beheadings. Whatever else."

"But he's got no record in the States?" I coughed hard into my elbow, took a deep breath after I finished. The sea air drifted up this way from the Embarcadero and I smelled salt and water and the long decay of fish. Somehow, I smelled Castaneda's body, too. Like I did the previous night.

"Nope," Slade said. "Castaneda's dressed up for Halloween."

Slade meant Castaneda was a ghost. I shrugged. "Okay, so he don't exist. But you got real people saying he's in the drug game."

"And he's up the chain."

"Castaneda gets some webos," I said. I placed a finger beneath my chin, acted all Sherlock Holmesian about it. "Castaneda tries to play superstar on his own team. But he ain't no all-star and the team captain chops him down to size. That sound about right to you? It's a stone cold who-done-it. But it's also a stone cold who-gives-two-shits. We get another CI to tell the same story and Captain Jackson lets this case go...Pushes it up to the feds, or DEA. Fuck if we care. Clearance rate stays savvy, baby."

Slade started moving down the sidewalk. I followed him. The deep-creased look gave way to another face—Slade wanted to know what happened beneath the bridge, and that meant this case was ours until some federal bureaucrat pulled it from Slade's cold, lifeless hands.

He said, "This has got to be more than all that, Frank. What drug lord is going to make a trophy of a sicario? I mean, on this side of the border? C'mon, partner. You and me both know this ain't just about a body in the bay."

A homeless woman in neon pink nylons and a purple windbreaker scratched her dirty head, asked us for a quarter. I reached into my pocket, but I shook my head when I didn't feel a coin. I like to make like I'm trying—in life there's lots of shit that goes for show.

Slade said, "You're a cold ass man, Frank."

"I didn't see you writing a blank check."

"But I don't pretend to write one."

I chuckled and said, "Whatever makes me feel better."

We kept walking and thinking. Soon, we moved out of the courthouse's shadow into streets drenched with sun and the clever brickwork of gentrification—goddamn condos called lofts and stores called boutiques.

Slade said, "This body is a fucking message. And we need to find out why. And to who."

"Look, listen to me, Skinny. I know you got all high and mighty when you did law school, but most of us are just getting along. You think I want to go and fuck around with some drug shit? The kind that hangs headless women from bridges and dips people in acid?" Part of me was messing with Slade, and he knew it. I wanted to put this murder down as solved. I believed in my job—I always did believe in my job. But another part of me was serious. It was the part that enjoyed breathing.

Slade said, "No murder makes justice a fool."

"And no fool gets away with murder," I said finishing the phrase.

Slade stopped. He looked at me with unblinking eyes. "There's something big behind this, Frank. I feel it, man. We got a drug man—high up, too—left like a Christmas gift beneath the bay bridge. No record except for what the streets say, and the man is mutilated on top of all that. I been a cop for too long to let that shit happen in my city. Fuck, I live here, Frank. I live in this fucking city and—"

"I live here, too. You know that, Skinny."

"So, what you going to do about it?" Slade watched me. His eyes were fat and dry. His skin stretched taut over a determined chin.

I said, "I'm going to find me the fool."

"Good. Any word about Jacumba and those supposed bodies?"

We reached a street corner, turned around and headed back toward the downtown station.

"Nothing I could find out, though I did talk to a prick of a retired BP agent."

"This prick give us anything?"

"A bad attitude. And..." I paused, thought about Candida's heavy breathing. "And the little bit of bullshit I need to believe we should check things out ourselves."

"Walk the fence line, you mean?"

"I guess so," I said.

"You drive, Slim Fat," Slade said. "On the way, I'll call the rest of my CI pricks. Oh, and we got the pics of Castaneda's body. I'll bring them with. Make a nice distraction during the drive."

Chapter 11

During the hour ride to Jacumba, Slade called his informants and got nothing about Castaneda. Nobody knew the man. Or, if they did, Castaneda scared them enough to keep quiet. Even after Slade promised the sicario was dead. The lack of information (and honesty) didn't surprise either of us. When it came down to it, the streets were a lot of shitty things: vengeful, dishonest, hate-filled, violent, forsaken, and hopeless. But the streets were also loyal to a code. And it was a code I could never fully shatter: The streets did not, under any circumstances, open up and talk to cops. The way you got people to talk, in my long years of experience, was to threaten them. You needed to use whatever threat you found might work, and you needed to use it well. After Slade hung up on his last call, I said, "Next boy we talk to about this is going to get smacked in the mouth."

I sensed Slade rolling his eyes. "I'll hide the tough guy routine until I really need it."

"Like right now, Skinny."

"You played tough on the girl last night?" He said it with a sarcastic question mark attached.

When I didn't answer, Slade slid some images from a manila envelope. These were the photos of Castaneda's body, taken by the coroner at the morgue.

Slade said, "That's a cartel tat, for damn sure."

He lifted the image so I could see it: The black inked rosary stretched down Castaneda's chest, ended—like I first thought—in a cartoonish image of Saint Death. Slade showed me other pictures, too: Castaneda's bullet wound, a gruesome close-up of his severed penis, a wide shot showing his severed hands laid out on a steel table.

"Nothing new," I said. "There's the tattoo, I guess. That's something."

"A thousand of those tattoos walking around, Frank. Especially if a guy spent time behind bars. Here, or in Mexico."

"You ever look into that—the Saint Death thing?"

Slade shook his head. "Not much. I just see it on the bad guys. I figure it's, like, a superstition. Like fucking fortune telling, you know?"

I nodded. Growing up Catholic, I still held a weird and unfounded reverence for religion, especially when I heard about saints. "You need to know who a man prays to," I said. "That'll tell you what he is."

Slade grunted. Too smart to believe in God, I supposed.

I checked my mirrors and shifted into the slow lane. Our exit for Jacumba was fast approaching. We sped through patches of manzanita, crossed a bridge high over a dry ravine. The highway headed downward, lost elevation at a rapid pace. Slade gripped the door handle, his knuckles white with anxiety. Slade was a bit of a control freak—he liked to drive.

"Surprised you wanted me to drive," I said.

"I'm trying to get over that thing." He stared out the

window, let his head fall back against the seat. "I can't always have control, Frank. Nobody can."

In my head, I saw Miranda plunging headfirst toward the black waters of the bay. No, I thought, nobody has control of a damn thing. Whole damn shebang is up for grabs. It always has been and it always will be. "You going to fly soon?" Slade hadn't been on a plane in three years. When a case forced us to travel, Slade either drove or, if it was too far, let me handle the long-distance stuff.

Slade chuckled. "Soon as I get my pilot's license, partner."

"Shit. Looks like you'll never see Cabo San Lucas."

"I can see it on the computer."

I shrugged, eased the car into a long curving exit ramp. We headed southeast on a two-lane road, passed scattered mobile homes and modest houses. Enough dirt bikes and old pickup trucks to make Texas proud. It surprised me to see that much horsepower here in California. I'm a city kid. I grew up three blocks from where me and Miranda bought our house. For this old cop, police choppers and traffic noise make familiar atmosphere.

Jacumba didn't have much of either.

We pulled into the small main street area, slid past a breakfast diner, three churches (two Catholic, somehow), a post office, and an elementary school comprised of beige, portable trailer classrooms. We came to a small park and pulled into the dirt parking lot. I got out first and Slade followed me. He came around the car and we both stared southward: In the distance, about two hundred yards away, the tall border fence stood glaring in the sunlight. Beyond it, clear as day, the territories of Mexico unspooled into blue sky and mystery. Slade sighed and I sneezed.

He said, "I'll take west, if you take east."

"You'll be walking into the sun."

"It's better for my tan."

As we walked through the desert—dirt, creosote and cacti—the fence's tapered ends revealed themselves. The fence ended on both ends after about a mile, maybe less. The metal posts stopped where the landscape became rocky hillside and carved ravine.

We reached the fence and I put my head between two of the posts, stuck it through. "My head's in Mexico, Skinny. How about that?"

"Funny, Frank. Be careful, or it'll get chopped off."

That brought me back over the border.

"Look for irregularities on the ground, bushes dragged or—"

"Exposed clothing," I said. "I know the deal." I looked down the fence line and squinted. "You know what, Slade? I'm wondering if our buddy Rambo overheard this business about the Jacoby family. Maybe he's dealing drugs, sure, but the kid's not passing his SAT, right? He's a low-level dealer. And I'm thinking he's trying to impress—or maybe scare—our angsty teen there."

Slade nodded and said, "Maybe wanted to impress the girl. Get himself a hand job."

I cringed, but added, "That seems—the whole idea—like it could make sense. What I'm saying is, maybe the shit about the Jacobys isn't bull honkey. Could be legit, and we're about to catch three more bodies."

"We'd hand it back to the feds."

I imagined working four murders at once, pushed back a wave of nausea. "True that, Skinny."

"Only way to find out is check it out. We find any-thing—I mean anything—we'll call it in, get a cadaver dog and organize a grid search."

"Man, I hope we don't find anything. If I got to see a dead kid, I'm going to lose my shit."

"Me too," Slade said.

The sun kept arching skyward. Dust entered my nos-trils and I sneezed twice more. The desert sounds didn't seem like sounds—creosote branches whispered against each other, a bird sang in discreet staccato, beads of sand toppled over each other in the half-existent wind. I sighed and ran a finger beneath my shirt collar. "It's getting hot," I said, but I didn't get an answer. I looked to my left and saw that Slade was already walking along his section of fence line, eyes to the ground, his head swiveling back and forth like a heavy machine gun.

I hoped like hell neither of us found a goddamn thing.

Chapter 12

You know what the wise men say: Hope in one hand and shit in the other—see which comes first. Or maybe it was George Burns who said that. Either way, it's more true than a bible story. I took my time walking along the fence. Sunlight burned high on my neck and I wiped sweat from my face. There were lots of boot prints out there—most of them military issue. Border Patrol agents stomping around outside their SUVs, waiting to punch the time clock. What a hell of a shitty job, I thought, sitting around for ten hours and not seeing a damn thing but dry-ass Mexico. Sure, agents sometimes chased migrants or stymied a drug shipment. But that kind of shit was few and far between—even they admitted that much.

I found a few cigarette butts, kicked them over with my toe. Marlboros, maybe. Me, I never smoked. Miranda did though. She liked a cigarette after a meal, after a workout, and after sex. Like cleansing your palate, I supposed. I tried to get her to give them up, but as I get older, I've found quitting a habit takes more time and effort than the habit itself draws. It's like drinking too much beer on the weekends: Fuck it, what else are you supposed to do?

The first time I met Miranda she was smoking a cigarette, in fact. Outside the old record store where El Cajon Boulevard hit the 805 freeway. Little place where they sold folk, blues and jazz albums from way back when—the best stuff to hit wax. She leaned one shoulder against a brick wall, her hair blowing in the breeze that came under the store's awning. In her left hand she held a record by James Brown and it was funny to see that, a teenage girl, in a short blue skirt and heels, holding an icon from a time before her time. Funny how we love music a generation or two behind. At least, those of us who have good taste love it that way.

She puffed on the cigarette, blew smoke at me from the corner of her mouth. I said, "Nasty habit for a lady."

"Who died and made you lord of the ladies?"

"I'm just saying."

She leaned both shoulders back against the wall, squared up to face me. "You think you're righteous enough to make it a law that a lady can't smoke?"

"That's up to the people and the courts."

She smiled and said, "What are you, the president?"

My heart burped a bit and I said, "I'm just an attentive social studies student."

"Got an A, huh?"

"B minus."

She laughed at that—my heart belched.

"I didn't mean to be a..."

"A man?" She lifted her chin and smoked some more, like she was doing it to piss me off.

I didn't respond to that, but instead moved toward the doorway, a glass swinging deal with posters of

Miles, Sinatra, Billie, and Elvis pasted to face the ceaseless traffic. Miranda's voice, like it did for so many years after that, stopped me from leaving her.

"You talk like a bureaucrat," she said.

"What's that mean?"

"All certain or whatever, like you read the rules in a manual."

"I'm just saying it's a bad habit. My fault for trying to help you out."

"What do you want to be when you grow up?" She tossed the cigarette to the sidewalk, stomped on it. Her eyes flashed on the busy street and swung slowly back toward me, touched my face with anger and delight.

I said, "I'm planning to be an LEO."

"A Leo? Like the astrology sign?"

"A cop," I said. "Law enforcement officer."

She laughed and I loved it—it was a melodic sound, edged with her sing-songy voice and a slight smoker's garble. Beautiful, somehow. Perfect. Miranda was all seduction and malice.

She said, "A Leo then. Mr. Righteous is going to be a Leo. You know what kind of people become cops?"

I shrugged. "The kind who want a steady paycheck and overtime."

Miranda spun away from the wall, twirled on one heel. She tossed her hair back over a shoulder, glared at me. "The kind who like to play bully, but can't do it without a pistol and some mace."

"Jesus," I said. "You are jaded to the bone."

"I'm just honest," Miranda said. "And forever will I be."

"You telling me, if I mugged you, you wouldn't want a cop to kick my ass?"

"No," Miranda said, "I'd do that myself."

I shrugged at the memory, walked a few more paces along the fence line. The sun was getting to me. I could feel the skin on my neck reddening, smell the heat boring into the ground and plants. It tasted like smoke and granite. I moved farther down, found more cigarette butts, a large empty water bottle. Nothing else. I moved a few yards from the fence, walked through the brush and dodged snake holes. After another thirty yards or so of walking, my cell buzzed in my pocket. I picked it up and said, "What's up, Skinny?"

Slade said, "I found something, Frank."

Hope and shit—those are mostly what we have as detectives. I turned and stared back toward Slade, saw him silhouetted in the far distance, an arm raised to draw my attention. "It ain't good," he said. "It ain't good at all."

"I can see you. Be there in a few minutes."

Slade said, "Take your time. This trouble ain't going nowhere."

Shallow graves don't give a man faith in humanity.

When I walked up on Slade, he was standing with his hands on his hips, staring down at a small section of upturned earth. I noticed dirt on his hands, dark crescents beneath his fingernails. His sunglasses covered his eyes, but I sensed the sadness there—wet trails streaked down his cheeks. A few feet away, at the base of a manzanita, a warm pile of vomit sat uncovered. Egg burrito re-cooking in the high noon heat. Slade didn't say anything to me. He cleared his throat, coughed without covering his mouth.

I stood behind him, looked down at the small section of upturned earth.

It took a second for me to see what Slade was staring at. The dark undersoil served as a bit of camouflage. And the hand was small—a child's hand. My eyes adjusted and I saw a red-painted thumbnail. The thumbnail led me to see the hand's shape. All bone. I saw four other tiny fingers, covered in soil, and a palm the size of an apricot. This led to a bone-exposed forearm, jutting from the ground like a buried wishbone. I felt nausea swirl in my belly. The burn stretched into my throat, like lava flowing over stone, and I turned to vomit. I went to my knees, retched, held the liquid in somehow. I pushed the vomit back down my throat, swallowed fire. "Jesus H. Christ, Skinny. What the hell are we into here?" I sat there on my knees, breathing hard and trying not to lose my breakfast.

"The goddamn kid was telling the truth," Slade said.

None of it made sense. Sure, we had to check out information like this, but most times it was a lie. Like everything else in this life. I remembered then that death is the final truth. The rest of this life is a mirage. Hell, life itself might be a projection of the mind, a reflection of imagination. Who knows? Why not? But death, that I knew—it took being a homicide detective for me to know—was a real fucking thing. Truth at its most brutal and final—no more fun and games. I struggled to my feet, moved next to Slade. He shook his head.

"You know, most times they call us in. We don't find the damn bodies. We just…"

"Yeah," I said. "I know what you're saying."

Slade slid his sunglasses up onto his head. His eyes began their cruel inventory of details.

I did the same with my glasses, began my own assessment of the scene. The grave was about fifteen feet from the border fence. Recent rain, it seemed to me, ran heavy there between manzanita and cacti. Slade exposed the child's hand, but the rain did its job, exposed an odd shape there between the desert foliage. I looked for shoe prints in the immediate vicinity, saw none except for those behind me and Slade. Our own path to ruin. I looked, too, for items forgotten by the gravedigger: cigarette butts, dirty gloves, broken branches, personal items. Nothing, of course. The body (more than one?) would be the source of any evidence. DN-fucking-A, the detective's French drop.

"No footprints," I said.

"No, sir." Slade turned and studied the border fence. He swiveled his gaze east and west. "Have to run a cadaver dog all along the fence, maybe up into the hills, too."

"Sheriff's department might want this one."

Slade looked back at the hand. "God, I fucking hope so."

"I guess we have a link to our cartel body though, huh?"

"Fucking Turner," Slade said. "And his pal, Rambo."

We stood in silence for a good long minute. I thought about Rambo saying he was a dead man. Looking at the little girl's lifeless hand, I imagined he was correct.

"You thinking again about the tough guy routine?" Slade did not like to play bad cop. Not because he couldn't do it, but because bad cop meant leaving bruises on suspects. It meant creative interrogation techniques. That was my area. Always had been, once I got my LEO edu-my-cation. I threw a nice punch, and I liked to throw it. I'd done worse, too. But that was something Slade and me didn't talk about.

Slade said, "I'm thinking Rambo needs to fess up. I don't give two fat shits how that happens, Frank. We need to find his ass before whoever-the-hell does." He sighed. "I got to go call this in." He turned around and walked back toward the fence, taking care to step in his previous footprints. Slade's shoulders slumped. He looked like an old crow in his leather jacket.

I stood there and stared at a dead child's dirty hand. At a dainty red thumbnail, the bone below it. For a long time I didn't think of anything. My brain was blank, dormant. It was like my life had been wiped clean, like I didn't exist. For those few moments, I was dead. I was nothing. I was a collection of molecules wiped away, dashed to pieces, driven to non-being. I was the reflection of my imagination of (non)life—I was nothing-ness.

But the heat weighed heavy on me. The smells—both imagined and real—of dirt, dried lizard shit, cacti flowerings, and degenerated flesh, burned my nostrils. I came back into myself—my real, live self—for another murder in another forgotten part of the world. I wasn't nothing. I was a murder detective. And I had shit to do.

Chapter 13

Back at the car, waiting for the sheriff's department to arrive, I said, "I might just need to call my daughter, see how she's doing."

"Make sure everything's okay," Slade said.

"That's right."

"I got people I can call too."

Here we were—two clichés talking like made-for-TV cops. I was a bit ashamed by it, aware how it took a traumatic experience for me to communicate—or try to communicate—with my own daughter. But I guessed the shame was something deeper than that, something tied to my own sense of masculinity and fatherhood.

Slade wandered off toward the highway. I leaned against the trunk of the car and dialed my daughter's cell number. Sometimes, in this job, you're witness to a deed that can't be undone—it puts you to being sentimental. Or...scared. That was it—sometimes you get scared. You call your wife, your girlfriend. Hell, you call your ailing mother. You just get the foreboding nature of death, the scent of it, right up your nose and into your head. It's rot. And it stinks.

"What, Dad?"

"Kimmie, I—"

"Can I call you tonight, Dad? I'm at work right this second." Her voice sounded garbled, but it wasn't the connection.

"Are you smoking those cancer sticks again, Kimmie?"

"Mom did."

Neither of us spoke. I stared at the desert and tried not to see the lifeless hand jutting from the dry earth.

I heard Kimmie sigh. "Dad," she said. "I didn't mean to—"

"It's fine. I just wanted to see how you were, how things are going."

"I'm fine, Dad. You know I'm fine."

"I don't know unless you tell me. How can I—"

"Are you lonely, Daddy?"

The way she said it put me in a state you don't much see from a grown man. I felt tears burn beneath my eyes. I blinked them away and took a deep breath, pushed my sunglasses higher onto my fat nose. Here I am, I thought, talking to my daughter while some kid decomposes in a shallow grave. Fucking inferno that is this life.

"I take that as a yes, Dad."

"I miss your mom. So, if that's what you're asking..." I didn't finish my thought. I turned to see Slade pacing beside the highway, his cell pressed to his ear. I wondered if he was talking to the reporter. Not the best idea, but if they were in love...

"Have you thought about...dating?"

This snapped me to attention. I felt a familiar rage tug at my throat, claw down into my chest, reach for my heart. "What the hell do you mean? It's only been—"

"Not for love, Daddy. And not because you didn't

love her. Just because it's nice to be with somebody now and then. That's all I mean by it. Mom wouldn't want you to be alone."

I said, "Then why'd she kill herself?"

Kimmie started crying. It began with a slight whimper, but became a light weeping. Soon, her voice seemed caught down in her knees, struggling to surface over her emotion. "I'm just trying to help you, you fucking asshole."

"Kimmie, I—" The line went dead and I finished my sentence, "I wanted to say, I love you." But nobody heard me. I looked over at Slade. He lifted his chin at me and wiggled his phone in the air. More calls to make. I waved back and dialed the number for ex-Border Patrol agent Hector Candida. His voicemail clicked on after two rings. Motherfucker silenced me. His message said he might call you back if you left your name and number. When the line beeped, I said: "Hector. Hola, amigo. It's your new best friend, Detective Frank Pinson. SDPD. We talked earlier today. I have some news, my friend. Need you to give me a call. Soon as you can. And Hector, don't try and fuck with me. I don't like to get fucked with—I promise you that."

As I hung up, a sheriff's deputy pulled into the parking lot, flashed his sirens for no apparent reason, and parked in front of me. I looked back at Slade. He was already walking toward us.

"Every once in a while it happens," Deputy Markson said. "We get ourselves a dead Mexican. What they do is try to cross the border and they die of thirst, hunger... Shit, pure desperation."

He was a slope-shouldered white man of some thirty years, widening at the hips, but with no strength or agility. I stared plain-faced at him. I didn't like him from the moment I shook his soft right hand. I imagined his diet of TV dinners and cheap light beer, a scoop of ice cream (or four) every single night. Maybe I was too harsh on deputy Markson.

He said, "I tried to tell the congresswoman we got to make this fence electric. She came out here for a town hall and the LT said we should go on and see her, advocate for blue lives. You two see it, don't you? It's easy to see how—"

I cleared my throat to cut him off. "You keep your politics to yourself, big boy. How about you check on the techs, see when the hell they'll be here?"

Slade stared in silence at the deputy. He didn't like the man either.

"Jesus to pieces," said Markson. "You two are real city boys, huh. Serious as all hell. I understand it—last thing you want to do is wait around here while all that big important stuff happens in the city. I bet you got a whole bunch of—"

"Make the call, Deputy," Slade said. "Do it before I shove that baton up your ass."

There was no more discussion. The deputy went around his car, climbed inside, and spoke into his radio. The feelings were mutual—he didn't like us either.

As it should be, I thought.

Two minutes later, my old buddy Lengo pulled into the parking lot in his cruiser. He gave me a man-hug and pumped Slade's hand. "Nice to see you again, Skinny. You still run around with the fat man here, huh? Thought you might shoot his ass on purpose."

71

Slade said, "I think about it every single day." He patted the 9 mm holstered on his hip. "It's why I keep old Bessie loaded."

I rolled my eyes and asked Lengo about deputy bumblefuck. "Who the fuck is this asshole, Lengo?" The guy was still in his cruiser, mumbling into the radio.

"Markson? He's…" Lengo stopped talking, peeked over his shoulder to make sure the man couldn't hear. "His family owns a bunch of land out here. They're old railroad money, Frank. Rumor is they're trying to get the old rail line back up running, move goods from Tijuana into the Midwest, vice versa."

Slade said, "I read about that in the city paper. They had a rail route down into Tecate and westward, went out of business because—"

"Company that owned it couldn't keep it going," Lengo said. "Markson's daddy bought the rights. Been twenty some odd years and they can't get the permits to update the line, get a new locomotive on there and tugging profit back north. Sonny boy over here is more capitalist pig than cop. He's about as much cop as—"

I lifted my finger to my lips as Markson pulled himself from the cruiser. Lengo turned to salute him. "You find out what's what, Markson?"

"Hey, Lengo. Techs will be here any minute. They got some feds headed out here, too. Not sure why. It's probably just another migrant came over from—"

I said, "You talk anymore shit about that dead kid over there and I'll put you down my goddamn self."

Everybody got grim. Nothing but silence.

We stood there in the hot sun until the feds arrived.

Nobody said a fucking thing.

Chapter 14

It was the Jacoby kid. Like we feared.

And once the sheriff's cadaver dogs got out there, it was the whole family. Mom, dad, and daughter. The techs ID'd the bodies from fragments of clothing and, in the parents' case, by actual ID. Not official yet—they'd need dental records for that. But enough proof to make the assumption. Didn't seem like the gravediggers were trying to cover up much. No noticeable trauma. The bodies were too decomposed for us to be sure, but it looked like a nonviolent death for all three. Well, other than the dying part.

Maybe suffocation. Is suffocation nonviolent?

Maybe in this crazy world.

Lengo took off once the feds arrived. Me and Slade spent the day walking from one grave to the next, assisting a G-man named Xander Dames with his documentation. His partner, a lady in tight Levi's named Tracy Atkins, knocked on doors around town. Within a few hours, it felt like me and Slade were minor players in a surreal stage ensemble—techs in white suits marked evidence with numbered flags, uniformed deputies waved looky-loo traffic past on the highway, cadaver dogs and their handlers searched in a widening grid, local TV news vans arranged a tight huddle, and Xander Dames sauntered from one grave to the next with his black tie flung over his shoulder, a notebook clasped to his hip.

I told Dames and Atkins about Hector Candida, about the teenagers giving us the tip on the bodies, about the dead cartel man named Castaneda (our murder, dammit), and about our runner, Rambo. Dames told us to find Rambo if we could, and to call when Hector Candida got back to me. Otherwise, they'd start a search for Candida if it seemed warranted. For now, it was coincidental.

I got the sense Dames and Atkins knew who killed the Jacobys, that maybe they were running through the motions. But those motions meant a lot of work. Three bodies in the desert means the whole world stops for a detective, a legit detective that is. I didn't know about these two: Dames seemed to ring a false note of gung-ho with his aviator glasses and goatee, and Atkins I didn't see much of—she ran off after shaking my hand.

When the sun hit the western hills, me and Slade hopped in the department-issue Ford Focus and drove out of town. Nobody said a damn thing to us. As we got on the highway, Captain Jackson buzzed my cell phone. "This is Frank, Captain. What's up?"

"You two headed back to the city yet?"

"Just got on the road."

Me and Slade shared a look—it was rare for the captain to call after regular business hours. As good as he was—and he was good—Jackson was a time clock jockey, counting the days until retirement. And a great pension. Like a lot of cops, sometimes Jackson just didn't give two shits. But when he did, you were in for decent overtime pay.

And a whole bunch of missed sleep.

Jackson said, "Don't go home. Stop and get some strong coffee. We got a gangbanger in here who has some info for you two. You're going to want to pick his brain. Sweet little guy with some face tattoos and a bullet scar on his neck."

"He there about Castaneda?"

Jackson grunted. "That's right. Walked in here about twenty minutes ago. Said he wanted to speak with Detective Frank Pinson."

"This OG have a name?"

"Said they call him Chato on the streets. Doesn't want to give his Christian name. We're working on it right now. I guess he forgot we have to do paperwork."

"Chato, huh?" I looked over at Slade and saw he was only half-watching the road. Get Slade a lead and he'll rip it to shreds. He accelerated and moved into the fast lane. I double checked my seat belt. "Kind of a wimpy name for a gangbanger, Captain."

"He said there's a reason for it, but it'd probably get him in some shit. With us."

"He's serious," I said.

"As a tax man's wardrobe. Got some weird joo-joo beads around his neck or something. Grim Reaper-looking pendant on what looks like a rosary necklace. I don't know what the fuck. Just get back here as soon as you can."

We hung up and I stared out the window at a string of endless taillights, all overtaken by the Ford's hardworking four-banger.

Slade said, "He got something for us?"

"Some G who wants to talk about Castaneda, a sweetheart named Chato."

"No shit," Slade said. "Chato, huh? I know that motherfucker."

I said, "He one to talk to the cops?"

"Not unless he's got a good reason—a selfish reason."

"Jackson said he's wearing joo-joo beads. Said it was religious. A pendant."

Slade nodded and said, "Saint Death. The narco saint. There she is again."

"She keeps on coming up, now doesn't she?" I scratched my chin, tried to keep my eyes open against the wave of fatigue.

"Fucking cult," Slade said. "Easy to sell snake oil to the poor, Frank."

"A cult, just like the Mormons," I said, laughing at my own joke.

"Right, Frank. just like the Mormons. And Catholics."

I glanced at him with cold eyes. But after a few seconds, I thought: Yep, like Catholics. Just like the Catholics.

When me and Slade entered the interrogation room, Chato had his boots on the table. Thick-soled cowboy boots made from some kind of exotic greenish skin. Gator boots, I thought. He wore a light gray guayabera and tight-fitting black Levi's. Not quite the gangbanger image I had in mind, but the captain was right about the tattoos. Chato was inked across his neck with Gothic lettering, on his head with Aztec warrior imagery, and he had three tear drops inked on his face. The "joo-joo" beads did, in effect, comprise a black rosary—slightly oversized—with Santa Muerte in place of the Virgin Mary. Imagine this pretty picture, would you?

Chato didn't make a move as we sat down, but instead shot us full of holes with dark, hate-filled eyes. He crossed his arms, lifted his chin in the manner of gangsters from in or around California and the Southwest, and said, "You finally my man, Frank Pinson?"

"I'm Detective Pinson," I said while taking a seat across from the gangbanger. "And this is my partner, Detective Slade Ryerson."

Chato said, "I know you." He was looking at Slade. "You're that street narco from the southeast."

Slade nodded. "How you doing, Chato?"

Chato ignored Slade and looked at me. "I'm supposed to talk to you."

I said, "That's fine, mister…"

"Call me Chato."

"Alright, Chato. That's fine. But me and Slade here, we work all our cases together. I'm just going to tell him what you tell me, or he'll watch it on the closed circuit." I motioned at the tiny camera hanging in the room's corner.

Chato shrugged, sniffed. "Tell those homeboys to turn the camera off then. Or I'll walk out of here."

I nodded at Slade. He left the room. Me and Chato stared at each other. Slade came back after fifteen seconds or so and took his seat.

He said, "We're all good."

"Okay, then. What can you do for us, Chato?"

"You got a murder yesterday, I heard."

I leaned back in my seat, crossed my own arms. "Who'd you hear that from?"

"Shit, streets are talking about it already. I heard you guys put it out there anyhow."

Slade said, "Trying to find out who the man belongs to—that's all."

"Next of kin, eh?" Chato smirked. He lowered his boots to the dirty, tear-stained carpet, leaned on the table. "Look, the thing is…I'm Enrico's people."

Slade said, "Castaneda is your brother?"

"Simón."

"What did you want with me?" If Chato wanted to claim his brother—fine. But he mentioned talking to me. That was the crux of the issue here.

Chato said, "I'm supposed to tell you that it's over with now."

"What is?"

"The bodies. No more bodies coming."

"Did you kill your brother?"

Chato shook his head—no. "My brother got what he deserved. For what he did. You know, these streets got mean revenge. I can't take that away."

"Who told you to come here?" I heard a strained anger in my own voice, felt it hum in my throat.

Chato tapped the pendant in the center of his chest. "Santa Muerte. In my prayers."

Slade chuckled. "The cartel did your brother and you're here to tell us to let it go. That it won't happen again. That something went wrong, and maybe that's why he got done here."

Chato shrugged. "I'm not saying nothing about no cartel. That's how you end up with your webos in a jar, no?"

Me and Slade looked at each other—fucking streets did talk.

Chato said, "I'm saying I'm here because of prayers. What I want, it's to take my brother home."

"And where the fuck is home for you?" My anger simmered, boiled.

"Chiapas."

Slade said, "You're so far from home. Tell me what it is to know your brother's dead. That doesn't make you want some revenge? I hear there's a code for you, for people like you."

Chato's chair creaked. "It's nothing to be far from home when you have a pistol. Maybe a machine gun in the trunk."

I said, "Should we follow you and take a look?"

Chato rolled his eyes. "You think I'm stupid? You're the one who's stupid, Detective. You don't even see things like you should. You believe in nothing."

"Who the fuck," I leaned close enough for Chato to smell my breath, "do you believe in? Some bullshit folk saint?"

He laughed and said, "What do they call you? Hard-boiled, right? That's what this is? From those little books at the farmacia."

Slade cleared his throat. "If this wasn't the cartel, who?"

Chato shook his head again, looked at us like we were, as he said, stupid. "How many Mexican guys you know run shit in Los Estados Unidos? Tell me that. Maybe I can answer it for you: None that I ever seen, amigos. Like I said it before: No more bodies." He raised his eyebrows. "Can I take my brother home now?"

"Back to Chiapas?" I sighed and knew I wanted to follow this motherfucker wherever he went. Mexico sounded good, but maybe not that far south. Too long a trip. Too hot. Too this, and too that. God, my eyelids wanted to shut down tight.

Chato added, "Shit. My brother was an anchor baby. He's from Oxnard."

Slade tapped the table with his thumbs. "Your brother, did he—" His eyes prodded at the pendant around Chato's neck.

Chato fingered the miniature saint, studied it for a long time. "She'll answer all your questions, you know? But sometimes...Even our saints can fail us." When his eyes lifted and settled on us again, I saw the slightest tinge of grief.

I said, "They cut off your brother's fingers, too."

"With his junk," Slade said.

Chato's facial expression didn't change in the way we hoped. Plain-faced and without sadness, he said, "It's what you get for stealing. Can I take those pieces home, too?"

My turn to laugh. "Just the man's dick," I said. "We never found the fingers. No te preocupes, Chato—it's not too much to carry."

Chapter 15

The case I think about most—the one that made me a real murder police—was the first case I worked alone, before Slade got his promotion. It was a senseless beating down in the Gaslamp District. An accountant visiting from Minneapolis got twisted up with a couple navy cadets after a night of drinking and dancing.

What I found out, from assorted witnesses and two pieced-together surveillance tapes, was that the navy guys thought the accountant was hitting on them. Sure, he ran around with some effeminate mannerisms and a pink polo shirt, but that didn't make the man a sexual predator. On one tape, from a camera outside the club, I saw the accountant shake hands with one of the cadets. The other cadet, a tall kid with his navy buzzcut and prominent biceps, walked over and pushed the accountant. It came out in court the accountant asked them back to his hotel room for a drink. Mr. Seaman decided to defend his masculinity by shoving the accountant into the gutter. From there, it was a stompfest—Doc Marten boots do a good job when it comes to breaking facial bones. Or maybe it was the hatred inside the Seabees.

Either way, Mr. Accountant ended up with a crushed

skull and permanent brain damage—until he died, that is. I still remember watching him in the hospital room. All those wires attached to him, and those monitors beeping like a chorus of mechanical heartbeats. Odd thing, to see a man pass from this world into the next. And all because he liked the company of other men. All because two small town losers couldn't deal with that. My stomach turned when I thought about it. I'm no activist, but when you work homicide you see every heartbeat as a small miracle to protect. And when one gets snuffed out—for no goddamn reason—it makes you murderous yourself.

About six months after I booked the two navy punks for second-degree murder, the accountant's father called me. He was an ex-janitor with a Midwest accent. He thanked me twice for doing what I did for his son. And then, for the next ten minutes, he sobbed.

What do you do with that?

Keep solving murder cases—that's what.

Even when, and if, the victim is a cartel sicario, or a gangbanger, or an entire wealthy family.

I sat at my desk and stared at the images of Enrico Frederico Pablo Castaneda's dead body. In an email, the coroner said the tool most likely used on the man's hands and Johnson was, as Slade posited, a set of semi-sharp garden shears. Bolt-cutters would have been more humane.

I stared at Enrico's bloody face for a long time. What was behind those glazed brown eyes? What kind of man gets himself chopped up and stuffed in an oil drum? But worse than that, what kind of man does it take to give the order: Chop Enrico's dick off. His fingers, too. Dump him in the bay. And beyond that, what kind of man sends a message to the murder police that they should drop the case? Hell, to me, that's the kind of man who needs to get got himself. These reasons, among others, were what kept me up at my desk. And Slade, too.

From his desk beside me, Slade said, "I bet the son-of-a-gun who did this is American."

"Enrico's American. Or, shit, he was. Not sure if citizenship transfers to heaven."

"But, I'm saying…" Slade sighed. "Maybe it's more than drug business. Maybe it's something besides that. More than that."

I stood, walked over to the small coffeemaker in the center of the office. I poured a fat cup and sipped it down by half, refilled. No cream. No sugar. Just bitter black tar and unanswered questions. I said, "Think about the Jacoby family: How's that lead to this?"

Slade started tapping at his computer keyboard. I walked over to my desk, fell into my wobbly chair. Everything squeaks in an empty office. The night detectives—Rombauer and Radicchio—decided to get some pasta and meatballs. They'd been at their candle-lit dinner for the past few hours. I guessed they found their way to a dive bar.

I didn't blame them.

I was on my way to that, too. If Slade didn't stop me.

Everybody else was home for the night.

Slade said, "You know Jacoby was on that stadium committee?"

"That bipartisan thing…What was it, trying to get a new stadium measure passed?"

"Right," Slade said. "Here it is." He clicked his mouse and a website popped up—the local newspaper.

"They wanted to take that land downtown, level a bunch of low-income housing complexes. Little immigrant neighborhood, too. All these old houses from the '40s."

"Sure," I said, remembering a series of news headlines from a few months prior. "Lots of those post-World War Two houses. And they were saying it'd all be paid for. No taxes. But wasn't it…"

Slade grunted, studied his computer screen. "They wanted the city to purchase the northern half, resell it to some developer for a song. Fucking pennies on the dollar. Mixed-use housing and economic development, they said. But for some reason…"

I rolled my chair to Slade's desk, read over his shoulder. "P&J Associates."

"Yes, sir."

I thought for a minute, tried to envision the bit of land referenced by the news story. I knew the location, but I didn't have the northern part in my head. "We might run over there, check out this part they wanted to pass to the developer. Wonder what that's all about."

"Bay views?" Slade scratched his head.

"You think?"

"Could be," Slade said. "If you build things right."

I finished my coffee, sucked air through my too-sensitive teeth. "The hell does Jacoby have to do with Castaneda?"

"It's this," Slade said.

"Drugs and property. These aren't the same sport, are they?"

Slade cracked his knuckles. "You can't look at it like that, Frank. The sport…it's making more fucking money. That's the sport. Get. That. Money."

I thought about the accountant, how he died with all those tubes plugged into his body, weird machines beeping and humming all around him. Was that it for the man—did counting money make him human? God, I sure hoped not. Because if it did...Shit, that about reached the boundaries of my intellectual capacity. I erased the idea from my head.

"You up for a walk in the city, Slade?"

Still squinting at the news article, Slade said, "Why the hell not?"

While we walked to the car, Slade got on his cell to QB. The young buck was back following Turner, our teenage wastelander, but there wasn't much to report. The kid spent a lot of time at a head shop down off Market Street, near the plaza mall. He had a part-time job with a three-man moving company, and he smoked weed down at Seaport Village, where the tuna boats came in—that was about it: the stoner's cycle. Slade told QB to stick with the kid for one more day, see what happened. After that, QB's overtime—sad to say—was maxed out for the month.

Chapter 16

We drove fifteen blocks or so southwest on surface streets, parked next to a shuttered automotive shop called Barney's. The sign out front said: Your car passes smog or we fix it for free. I laughed when I saw it. "Look at this, Skinny. You think anybody fails a smog test in this part of town?"

Slade came up beside me, straightened his shirt collar, and chuckled. "Nice workaround for an oppressive law, huh? Just like a brown paper bag for a forty."

"Some laws are stupid—isn't that the fucking truth?" And hell, I believed that with every cell in my big body. Nothing like a stupid law to make a lawman grin. Sometimes, though, stupid laws are useful. Like when you want to pull somebody over and get a look inside the car. Or maybe press somebody when they least expected it. We left the auto shop and sauntered along the sidewalk. Slade chirped the car alarm, pointing the key fob over his shoulder.

This neighborhood—one I knew—was true blue collar. It used to hold a large population of fishermen and their families, before the tuna industry got shot to shit by globalization. Now, it was a few square blocks of tiny houses with wrought-iron bars on the windows, broken curbs lined by secondhand pickup trucks with Baja license plates. Immigrant families piled into two- and three-bedroom homes, piñata remnants strewn across yard after yard. In the distance somewhere, we heard Mariachi music and lingering laughter.

As we walked, the ocean breeze touched us, but it was like a whisper in the night. I saw how the cityscape blocked the bay views here, though the neighborhood was some thirty or forty feet above sea level. I imagined the area back before skyscrapers and condo buildings dotted the horizon—it might have been the best view in the city: soft-rolling streets angled westward, moving down into flat city with the wide blue ocean forming a backdrop. But like a lot of things that are good for regular people, rich men got involved.

Corporations. Companies. Capitalists with a capital C.

Downtown, where the fancy people played, you had your bank buildings and condos, your fancy hotels and rooftop night clubs. I shrugged this off, too. You can't expect your world to keep being what it is, or what it always was.

Every single second an old idea dies.

Stop grieving for what doesn't exist, I thought.

We reached a corner store and Slade put his hands to an exposed bit of glass on the barred front window, tried to see inside the place. "Closed down for the night. I guess everybody already did the nightly beer run."

That figured. It was about thirty minutes past midnight. Long past the workingman's bed time. "This cross street here," I pointed ahead at K Street, "is where the north half of the property boundary starts. At least, when you look at the map." I pulled out a web-printed map on Xerox paper, unfolded it. I'd outlined the northern property area—the desired city seizure—with a yellow highlighter.

Slade took the map from me, studied it. "Looks like you're right. Runs three blocks up to Island Ave. And, let's see, maybe four blocks wide?"

Along K Street, the houses were similar. Square after square of fenced in yard. Simple, nice-looking houses set back from the street. I noticed lots of tinfoil covered windows and beware of dog signs. Also present were fútbol team banners and Mexican flags. Lots of well-tended flower beds and abundant gardens with bulbous red and orange peppers dangling like jewelry. Again, status quo in a blue-collar neighborhood. Back in the day, this was gang territory—tied up tight by the usual colors. Things had changed as the gangs moved east and south. Now it was—from the crime reports—all working-class crime. Your domestic disputes, paid for sex, and auto theft. Like my own neighborhood.

Beside me, Slade said, "Look at this, Slim Fat."

Next to us, outside a house surrounded by a low cinder-brick wall, there was a shrine. Sure as shit, it was a small statue—about knee high—mirroring the pendant on Chato's necklace. Saint fucking Death. The female face was half rubbed away, the other half shaded by a hooded cloak. She carried the reaper's scythe, and her female form was clear of dust or mud. There were unlit candles next to the statue, and a few dried roses, stiff gray petals scattered like confetti. "There's our totem, huh? What'd you say about her? She's the—"

"Narco saint. Or one, at least." Slade said. He had his notebook out already and I watched him jot down the license plate number from a lowered Chevy pickup truck parked in the yard. The house was dark. Slade jotted down the address—5743 K—and slipped his notebook back into his coat. Down the street, maybe a block and a half, I saw a shadow pass through the scattered light of the street lamps.

"What's that?"

We both watched as a teenager on a BMX bike weaved down the street, reached us after a few seconds. He stood on the pedals and coasted past us, his chin lifted in defiance. As I swiveled my head to watch, I heard him call out to the neighborhood: "Five-Oh in the house."

Slade grunted, shook his head. "Little punk."

"Another young scholar with high-level powers of observation," I said. Me and Slade had different ideas about kids. Slade got pissed off when kids talked shit to us. He took it as a sign of true disrespect. It was personal for him. Me, I took it as kids being kids. You can't get mad at them for doing what daddy does, can you? If it's real bad, you can. But still...I said, "Not like they didn't know we were here."

We turned right—that's south—down Twenty-Sixth and I spotted, over three blocks, five more Santa Muerte shrines. We rounded a corner and headed west. "Looks like we got ourselves some religious folks out here, huh?"

Slade shook his head. "That, or they like them some tasty superstition."

"Makes sense that Castaneda came from around here, right?"

Slade said, "Could be. His driver's license put him in Arizona though."

We put Tempe PD on hunting down Castaneda's

address. I expected them to call the following morning. Funny, to have an Arizona license, but to have your brother come in and ask to pick your body up in San Diego. We'd guessed the address was just a place for Castaneda to have documents sent. Get yourself a buddy with an AZ address and you don't have to renew your license for a long, long time. We saw this a lot with people who eventually had California warrants. That said, Castaneda was clean here in Cali, from what the system told us.

We passed a trio of growling pit bulls. Their lower jaws dripped with spittle and their yellow teeth clanged against a metal enclosure. I said, "Castaneda lives here, maybe. We don't have a known address for Chato?"

"Nope. He's not registered to vote neither."

"How in the hell does he do jury service then?"

Slade laughed, pointed at a handwritten flier nailed to a telephone pole. "The fuck is this?"

It was an old flier, the text almost faded from the sun. But I could still make out the letters. It said: Meeting in Opposition of Bond Measure 10! Come fight with Us! The same thing was printed in Spanish, just below the English. The date gave a Saturday a few months prior, and the location was a church a few blocks closer to the freeway—farther west.

"New Life Church," I said. "That's the church off Imperial there, near the freeway entrance."

"I know that one." Slade ripped the sign from the pole, folded it up and stashed it in a pocket. "Make a nice excursion in the morning. Get us some praying done. Aren't you due for confession, Frank?" Slade said it like a joke, but he wasn't being funny.

I decided not to play into his anti-religious sentiment.

I was Catholic, I thought, the fucking hell with it. If Slade wanted to go through his life so certain he was worm food, that was his pleasure—it wasn't mine. I preferred to believe in a higher power. It gave me something to look forward to—and it kept me sane after seeing my wife put in the ground. I wasn't up for any non-spiritual awakenings. "Look, Skinny...Forget about our body for a second. I'm wondering, you see anything here that says Jacoby?"

Slade shook his head, sighed, thought for a minute. "I see Castaneda, okay. We can knock on some doors about him. I see drugs, sure. Doesn't take a psychic to get that. Jacoby, I see him here for the land. But, shit, it's not like...I don't know," he said. "I guess I can see a land grab. Maybe that makes sense, but some people from the hood making a rich white dude take the dirt nap? That's a long shot for me."

"Always some kind of big money looking down at people, man. But here? Shit—I'm not sure it reads to me."

Slade said, "I'm with you," and spat onto the sidewalk.

I looked around at the fenced in homes, their wrought-iron bars a telltale sign of the neighborhood dynamic. I smelled incense and heard the endless chime of Mariachi still ringing on another block. A few dogs howled nearby and, farther north, I watched an airliner angle downward on its landing path. "Murder don't always make sense, Slade. You and me both know that."

"There it is," Slade said, nodding. "Another one of those stupid laws."

Chapter 17

Slade dropped me on the corner of University and 37th, a few short blocks from my empty house. We promised each other we'd get some sleep. But I knew I wouldn't sleep, not yet. I loosened my tie and pulled it over my head, scrunched it up and shoved it into a pants pocket. I never fancied myself a tie man, but you never know when, as a detective, you might need to look halfway decent. Last thing you want to do is notify next of kin about a murder with your fucking tennis shoes squeaking across linoleum. You learn that as a rookie. And you never fucking forget it.

I headed west a few blocks, feeling the good sea air coming inland, like a mist you can't see. My eyes felt funny and the lights from the streetlamps seemed to halo in my vision—I tried to remember the last time I got my eyes checked. I crossed an empty intersection without waiting for the light, noticed two blue tarpaulins spread out, lashed to a chain-link fence. Two pairs of bare feet stuck out like mummified limbs. The homeless in the city, since I was a kid, had gotten a whole lot worse. Problem was, nobody knew what to do about it. I sure didn't, but I made a mental note to bring some old blankets the next time I was down here. No matter where you wandered, sleeping outside got to be cold.

I kept walking down the quiet streets lined with cars and expired parking meters, the scattered trees looming above me like phantom limbs. And as I walked, I thought about my daughter. How she talked to me. How I talked to her. And I thought about that little girl buried out in the desert, her parents buried too, a whole family hushed up in shallow graves. Of course, that led me to my wife. But I knew, I forced myself to know, that Miranda took her own life. That was on her. And it might be on me. But my daughter and my son had nothing to do with it. They got dragged along, all the way into our shit, like that dead little girl. And that fueled the rage inside me. It ran hot as motor oil, thick and rapid in my veins, up through my neck—straight into my fat head.

On the next corner, with my anger closing down my vision even farther, I spotted the blinking green sign for Gia's, a cocktail lounge my wife used to enjoy. I hadn't been inside since the last time I went with Miranda. Fourth of July. We both drank margaritas, made small talk chewing roasted peanuts. I remembered an odd encounter that night: A slick dresser with a hooked nose came up to us, reached across me and took Miranda's hand. He said, "How do you do, Miss Miranda? Nice to see you."

My wife said, "Hey, Johnny. I'm good. This here is Frank, my husband."

And the way she responded to him, naming our relationship like a trail of bread crumbs to follow, made me uncomfortable. I'd never seen this man—Johnny with an accent on the "eee"—and he was too made up for the neighborhood. I clocked his loafers and slacks as high-end department store stuff, and his untucked blue button-down flowed like silk, though I suspected a much more expensive fabric. Whatever the hell that could be.

I reached out and shook his hand—no calluses. "How do you do, my man? I'm Detective Frank Pinson." I shifted a bit in the booth, knew the butt of my service weapon caught his eye. We stared at each other for a moment and I smiled.

Miranda said, "Johnny works over at the church center."

"Which church is that?"

"Bethel Church," Johnny said. He stepped backwards, glanced at my pistol before taking a long sip of Miranda's figure. "I run the youth congregation down there. We're off Sycamore Street."

"I know the church," I said. "Baptists." It rattled from between my lips like spittle. I couldn't help it—as a mal-practicing Catholic, I was a devout cynic, and a man forever caught in the erratic shadows of hatred. "You do some preaching, huh?" I finished my third margarita. Miranda's hand went to my thigh, squeezed.

"Oh, now and then," Johnny said. "I'm a preacher in training." He winked at Miranda.

Miranda said, "I bet you do just fine."

"We all got our work to do," I said.

He finished, "In the eyes of the Lord."

"How do you know my wife, preacher-man?" My smile felt hard as driftwood. I couldn't shake it, though I did feel Miranda squeeze my thigh again.

His eyes still fixated on Miranda, he said, "It was, what was it then? How we met?"

"Bake sale," Miranda said. "For the new organ you all got."

"Right. That's right."

I laughed, noticed the silence that followed.

"Well, Miranda. Nice to see you. And it's good meeting you, Frank."

"Detective Frank Pinson—I work homicide."

"I see," Johnny said and slipped away into the lounge's dark atmosphere.

Miranda yanked her hand from my leg. "Mr. Detective? What a fucking asshole you are, Frank."

"How well you know that guy?"

Miranda didn't answer. She sucked the rest of her drink through a neon green straw until it made a slurping sound. She rattled her glass of ice, slammed it down on the table.

I shifted in the booth, looked at her with eyes cut from years of criminal interrogation. "How well you know that guy? You going to tell me that?"

"You think, because you have a gun, you can treat people like shit?"

I sighed, shook my head in disgust. "That man's done time. I know from his walk."

"Oh, Frank," she said. "Fuck you and your thin blue line."

I watched her slim body ripple beneath her dress as she slid from the booth, walked past the old men slumped on their barstools, and exited the damp and dark lounge. Miranda only walked away from me one other time after that. I never followed. I never followed anything or anybody unless it had to do with murder.

And standing on a street corner in the dead city sounds of one in the morning, I thought hard about that—never following anybody or anything unless it had to do with murder. It was a sad thought for a sad lonely man. And I was standing in the middle of a sad lonely street. A few tow yards. An auto mechanic. Two tire shops. And this lone cocktail lounge—still open—called Gia's, a place my dead wife used to love. Again, my daughter's voice ran through my head, those thoughts she revealed about me being lonely.

And lost.

And maybe headed for the graveyard.

Thoughts like that didn't make me feel good. I don't care whether you wear a badge or an orange jumpsuit. If you don't have anybody, you don't have a fucking thing.

Ah, but maybe I was wrong. I had a dead man in an oil drum. I had a family of three, all of them put down for the dirtiest of naps. And I had Slade, too. Those were my people: All the dead, and the one man who believed, like me, that even the dead deserve a voice. I touched my piece, patted the spot where it lay snug against my hip. My badge was still clipped to my belt. I didn't consider removing it. I liked it there. I looked both ways down the empty street, crossed in the dark silence, and entered Gia's cocktail lounge.

Somewhere, behind me in the night, I forgot to bring my shadow.

Part Two

Chapter 18

In the morning, Slade was already in the office by the time I called him for a ride. I decided to walk the two miles to the station. When I got there, I had my tie over my shoulder, my sleeves rolled up, and sweat running off my skin like a Big & Tall swimsuit model.

Jackson stopped me in the hall, looked me up and down, and smirked. "You're in a bit late for a man working two homicides, Frank. You look like you've been in a sweat lodge." He smacked his lips—the captain liked his cherry-flavored Bubble Yum.

"Two bodies?"

"That's right," he said. "Just got the call that your amigo, Chato the sweetie pie gangster, is dead as a fucking non-nude strip club." Jackson smiled, blew a pink bubble. The bubble popped and he said, "But I got to ride your ass about something else first. Get the fuck in here."

I followed Jackson into his office. He motioned for me to sit down and I did. Behind his desk, on a shelf above some file cabinets, Jackson displayed ten softball trophies, all of them league championships. In my own silent way, I judged him for playing soft toss. But at least the man stayed active. "How'd Chato get done?"

Jackson lifted a hand, rotated it, and flipped me off. "Fuck you, Detective Pinson. Fuck. You."

"What the fuck did I do, Captain?"

Jackson shook his head, rotated his computer screen so I could see it, and tapped the space bar on his keyboard.

A video began to play:

At first, I saw only darkness punctuated by rapid flashes of neon—somebody moving forward through a dark space. Next, I saw a yellow light and, kind of blurry, a booth in a...lounge. It was Gia's—the camera moved closer. I saw my own large, round frame standing over the booth. My coat was on and my back was turned, but I recognized myself without question. In the booth, there were two women and, between them, a small guy with wet-looking hair and maybe, I couldn't be sure, a hooked nose.

I said, "Captain , I don't even—"

"Shut the fuck up and watch, Frank. You don't want to miss this."

My chair creaked beneath me as I shifted positions. A headache throbbed in my temple. The dregs of a hangover from a night I didn't remember. What I remembered was waking up on my bathroom floor, and staring down into the black hole where my toilet used to be. I also remembered the moist, rotting scent of liquor vomit.

On the computer screen, I saw myself reach toward my hip, pull my service weapon. The two women scattered, disappeared off screen. The man with wet-looking hair—I knew by then it was Johnny—started laughing, laughed so hard he put both hands on his belly and shook. And I saw myself, my back still turned, swing down and strike Johnny in the face with my pistol. I couldn't be sure, but it looked like a tooth or two sprayed from his mouth.

The camera shook, lost focus for a moment.

I looked at Jackson across the desk, my heart beating up into my throat. He had his eyes closed, two fat fingers pinching the bridge of his nose.

The video cleared, came into bright focus. I saw myself leaning over Johnny, screaming into his ear. His head was planted on the booth's table. His legs kicked beneath it, as if he was a child struggling to surface from deep water. My gun was still in my right hand and I lifted it, brought it down onto Johnny's head. The table shook. My big frame straightened, stood over the unconscious body before me. I looked once in each direction. I holstered my piece, turned around, and walked straight into the camera.

The screen went blank.

I said, "You can't hardly tell it's me, Captain."

"Can't hardly?"

"It's blurry."

"Frank, I don't give two shits if it's subtitled in fucking Cantonese. I know it's you. You know it's you. And whoever the fuck sent this video—to my fucking department email address, by the way—knows, sure as shit on shoe leather, it's you. It's fucking you. What I want to know: The fuck did this guy do to deserve a pistol-whipping from—"

"I don't remember none of that, Captain Jackson." I knew my eyebrows were arched high above my nose. This didn't look good. It didn't look right. Oh, and it was none of those two things.

"That's one thing I believe, Frank. Did you look in the fucking mirror this morning? You look like some kind of fucking...I don't know. You look like a red-faced fuckup who drank too much liquor and puked his guts down a black hole."

I didn't dare tell him he was right.

"Detective, this is a media clusterfuck waiting to happen. It's a crucifixion. What the—"

"Who sent the video? I'll go have a talk with him."

"Oh, right." Jackson laughed the laugh of a man long past his prime. Without humor. "You'll talk to him. You going to talk with your muscles again?"

"No, Captain. No, I just—"

"What you're going to do, Frank—Mr. Hardboiled Tough Guy—is exactly what I tell you. You're going to leave all this to me, you're not going to say another fucking thing. And, I swear by the devil as my fucking witness, you're going to solve these two murders. I want that red to go black before next week. That's all the fuck you're going to do. And if I catch—"

"That's only three days," I said.

"Does this look like the face of someone who gives a shit?"

It did not, but I didn't say so. Instead, I said, "You don't understand. That's the guy who—"

"Please, shut the fuck up."

I shifted in my seat again and pointed at the computer screen. "That's not admissible if—"

"Frank. Frank. Frank." The captain rotated his computer screen, punched a key. "I'm going to tell you one more time: Be fucking quiet. Like a mouse. You know what a mouse is, Frank?"

"Yes, sir. I know what a rat is."

"A mouse. Not a rat, Frank. A fucking mouse."

"A mouse," I said as somebody knocked on the office door.

Jackson said, "Come in."

The door opened and Slade's pretty boy face appeared. "Frank, there you are. Been calling you for an hour. We caught another one, partner. Where the hell have you been this morning?"

"Detective Ryerson," Jackson said. "I was just about to send your partner over. Fill him in on the details, would you? I'll see you both down at the scene." Jackson glared at me as I stood and followed Slade out into the hall.

We exited the building, jogged down the marble steps, and rounded the corner for the parking garage. I rolled down and buttoned my sleeves, left my tie slightly loose. The veins in my neck, like the previous night, surged with anger and blood.

Slade said, "What was that all about?"

"Forget it," I said.

Slade lifted his eyebrows at me, rolled his lips to one side of his face. "Can you forget it?"

I tried to remember something from the previous night—anything. All I saw was the blurred video image of myself, my moving arm, the big pistol coming down onto Johnny's wet-looking head. I grunted and said, "I already forgot it. I can't remember a fucking thing."

"I come out to the street—I'm hearing this homie scream bloody murder, right?—and there's a silver Benz parked with the low-beams on, two guys standing over homeboy and they're shooting his ass. Like, really

103

plugging homeboy with lead, right? Crazy ass shit, man—I'm telling you."

Beside me, Slade was writing all the details on his meticulous notepad. I looked this middle-aged Mexican guy up and down, noticed the low-slung Dickies and short-sleeved flannel shirt, buttoned to his throat. "You been inside, homie?"

"Man, the fuck kind of question is that? I'm out here talking to the cops and they're giving me shit. Why, because I'm fucking Mexican?"

Slade sighed and said, "The uniform, homie. We just need to make sure we're getting the best information. You know how it works."

The man guffawed, spat at our feet. "Why I know how it works? Because I'm fucking Mexican? That why, you punk ass cops?"

"Look," I said, "you're right—that's my bad. I got a lot on my mind, as you can imagine." I looked over my shoulder at Chato's body lying face up in the street, covered by a white sheet. Splotches of near-black blood soaked through the sheet. His gator skin boots poked out like a child's two front teeth. A crowd of neighborhood onlookers, cordoned behind yellow crime scene tape, stared at the body. A few women made the sign of the cross in futile repetition.

Jackson, hands on his hips, watched the techs gather and mark evidence. Slade was still catching up in his notepad.

I looked back at our witness and saw his eyes pasted on the body. "We're just going to need your full name, and we don't want to find out anything we don't know when—"

"You run my fucking name?" He lifted his chin at us,

straightened his sleeves.

Slade said, "We have to do it, sir. It's how it goes."

"Sir is goddamn right. Here I am trying to help your ass."

I shrugged. "You're helping him." I pointed my thumb over my shoulder. "Me, I could be sitting back at the office, drinking shitty coffee and watching Lakers Showtime highlights on YouTube."

"Ooh," our witness said, "Magic was the shit, huh?"

"Smooth ass James Worthy," I said. "High-flying Byron Scott."

"Don't forget Kareem, man. He big and slow, but he smooth as peanut butter."

Slade shifted as if bored. "You guys are too old school for me. I'm talking Golden State Warriors with Steph and Klay and—"

"Get out of here with that Bay Area shit," homeboy said. "This is So Cal, homie."

"That's right," I said. "Now, from one Lakers fan to another, what happened to our homie who isn't waking up from his nap?"

"Shit. They plugged his ass. And his body is all, like, shaking and shit—like he's being shocked, you know? They plug him so many times. I swear to God, man. It's like, motherfucker is dead. And I'm hiding right over there." He pointed at a small home on the street corner. The house was circled by a low wall in the manner of many surrounding homes. "They turn around and they get in the Benz. Fucking, gonzo…" He crossed his arms, stared at us with defiant certainty.

Slade looked up from his perfect printing. "You get a license plate number?"

"Hell no. Tell you what I saw though." He tapped

the side of his head. "The back windshield had a name on it, one of those stickers you get made. All white letters and it said, 'Juarez.' I know that for damn sure. Clear as day."

"You ever seen that ride before? Know the name?" I felt the hot summer air hit the back of my throat. I tried to watch homeboy's eyes for the clever glint of a lie.

He said, "Do I know the name? Of course I know the name, motherfucker. That's some narco shit, homeboy. You should be out here in a Halloween mask, make sure nobody knows you're murder police. Better believe that shit, too."

Slade shook his head, turned and walked back toward Chato's lifeless body. Behind me, I heard him say, "Fuck this bullshit."

"What, man? That dude thinks he's all fucking fancy, huh?"

"We don't get many drug murders in the city," I said.

"I don't know, homie. I see what I see."

"You saying the narcos are bringing that murder shit to me?"

He shrugged. "I don't know, man. You're the fucking detective. Maybe it's a family name, something sweet to make abuela proud. There you go—can I be your assistant now?"

I laughed and took down the guy's full name.

When I turned and walked toward Slade and Jackson, homeboy shouted after me: "Eh, fuzz! I did do some time though! Grand theft auto, motherfucker!" The remaining onlookers laughed and pointed at me.

When I reached Slade and Jackson, I could see they were both irritated. Jackson popped small pink bubbles and Slade kept flipping pages in his notepad.

I said, "Put that fucking thing away, Slade. Look around and watch all these motherfuckers." You'd be surprised how many times a homicide cop spotted a killer at a public crime scene. I'd done it three times over the years, all drug killings, but I knew it happened in white upper-crust suburbia too. Don't let the rich fool you. They're as violent and perverted as the rest of us—I think they're worse.

Jackson said, "This is a cartel hit."

"Maybe," I agreed. "We were down here last night and it was quiet as a shrine." Jackson looked surprised. "You two were down here last night? What the fuck for?"

"A hunch," Slade said, "about the Jacoby murders."

Jackson's cheeks got red. "So, you two wasted a whole day on that Jacoby thing?"

"It's part of the Castaneda murder," Slade said.

"The fuck it is. You know what solves homicides?"

Me and Slade shook our heads, sarcastic.

"Murder police who work their own fucking cases. That's what, motherfuckers. Jesus Christ."

"Well, we were right on the hunch." Slade waved his hand at the body like he was revealing the final turn in a complex illusion.

Jackson blinked. He stared at the body, looked back at the onlookers. "Fuck it," he said. "Just get me a fucking charge on these murders by Monday. I don't care if you pay a casting director to get you realistic witnesses." He paused, added, "And, yes, I'm fucking with you."

I said, "About the charge, or the—"

"The witnesses, asshole. Of all the cops in the city, Frank, you're the one who needs this most."

Jackson stormed to his car—he got the shiny Ford Taurus—and sped off without waving.

Slade smacked my arm to get my attention. "Frank, look who the fuck it is."

Way off down the street, riding a green BMX bike in small circles, was the punk kid from the night before. His head swiveled as he turned circles in the street, his gaze pointed in our direction.

Slade said, "You want to talk to him, or should I?"

As I was about to answer, my cell buzzed. I pulled it out and recognized the number—Candida, the former Border Patrol agent. "I got to take this," I said. "You go smack the kid around and get more information."

Slade didn't laugh, but he did start walking toward the kid. I took a deep breath and answered the call.

"I don't know jackshit about those bodies, Detective. Reason I'm calling you—it's to get my name out of your mouth. I'm trying to be real here." Candida said this with the false confidence of the powerless. Behind it all, he was scared. He cleared his throat more than necessary, and tried to fill the silence before I responded. "If those bodies got there after I—"

"I don't think you killed anybody, Hector. What I do wonder, though, is why you got out of the Border Patrol business. That's the big thing here for me. I mean, shit, you say—"

"I took some money from a drug mule." He said it plain, without regret.

"You what?"

He cleared his throat—that was four times in thirty seconds. "I took some money from a drug mule, but it's not what you think. It didn't go down like they say, man."

"So, tell me, how'd it go down?" I watched the on-lookers behind the crime scene tape while Candida talked. All the women crossing themselves reminded me about my prayers. I promised myself I'd say some Hail Marys and Our Fathers before the weekend ended. I treated prayer like I treated dental hygiene—you hate it, but you have to do it.

"I used to work down near Tecate, across the border," Candida said. "The thing is, one day, I get put on a checkpoint, just north of the border. Near Jacumba, on the highway."

"I know the spot." Every few hundred miles, the Border Patrol set up checkpoints. I knew it as a way to—in the worst possible sense—stereotype drivers and detain them. Like most efforts at racial profiling and bias, it worked real fucking well. Talk about the American way.

"But I'm not on the checkpoint, okay? That's just a way for us to get the real drug runners to try to skirt the checkpoint. Like, they'll use the highway and get off a few miles before...walk through the desert."

"So, you patrol north and south," I said.

"Right, but it's only me that day. My partner got the runs and I'm out there by myself, pissing yellow steam and praying I don't step on a baby rattlesnake."

"So the fuck what? It's your job." Behind a group of old women, I noticed a black cowboy hat appear. The hat maneuvered through the crowd, pressed toward the crime scene tape.

"So, I'm in this ravine, more like a box canyon, and I'm headed down, trying to get to a spot where I can see better. Next thing I know, I hear voices—Spanish. I try to get my gun out, but then I hear two voices telling me not to move. I wait for a second and three guys carrying big ass marijuana bales come through. They've got the fucking things on their backs and the dudes are sweating. I'm talking slave labor here. Next thing I see, I got two assault rifles pointed at me. These two fuckers—scouts, I guess—are standing above me on the canyon walls."

The black cowboy hat moved faster through the crowd, got closer. I started watching it for real then. I thought it might be somebody coming to see their fine craftsmanship. "And they said they'd kill you if you didn't take the money, am I right? That you were on the payroll and—"

"That's what fucking happened, man. And I went right to my supervisor, called that shit in and they got there and the shit just went—"

The black hat was one row behind the yellow crime scene tape. "But you didn't say a damn thing about the money, did you?"

"What am I going to say, I took ten grand so I didn't get my brains blown out? How's that sound? Think about it, man…The fuck am I supposed to do?"

"Isn't that the truth? You took the money because you had to?"

"They're not going to buy that shit, man—I know that and so do you."

"You should have told them about the money," I said.

Candida cleared his throat a final time. "They knew. It was a fucking DEA sting and how the fuck was I supposed to—"

"Candida," I said. "Let me call you back."

"Don't you expect me to answer you again, man. Oh, hell no, I'm not—"

I hung up and watched as the black cowboy hat appeared in the front row. It was a guy dressed like a vaquero, though I doubted he'd broken many wild horses. He wore slick cowboy boots, the requisite ten-gallon hat, tight white Levi's, and a nice long-sleeved shirt. He had a thick black mustache and it was spread wide into a grin. He lifted a cell to his chest, held it out in front of him—the fucking phone was pointed right at me. I motioned at the nearest street cop, waved like a crazy person, yelled, "Get your ass over here! Look! Grab that fucking cowboy! Get him before—"

Chapter 19

Slade said, "He got your fucking picture, didn't he?"

I nodded, scanned the scattered onlookers. The vaquero was gone, vanished behind the sea of people. After yelling at him, I rushed through the crowd flanked by two patrolmen, but the old ladies and kids and stern-mouthed men refused to step aside. We got mired in a whirlpool of taunts and bodies, spun around by the neighborhood's distrust of authority and silver badges. By the time I waded through the crowd, the vaquero in the black cowboy hat was gone. Smirking at Slade, I said, "They want to know who I am, where I live, they can find out."

He didn't seem so sure. "We don't make our shit public, peddle it to the press."

"You're wrong about that, Skinny." I glanced at the street corner, where K met Thirtieth—we'd pushed the crime scene back that far to limit the crowd's view and scattered heckling. I wanted to get another look at the body before we transported it to the coroner's office, and I didn't need the entire neighborhood taking in the scene. But there was a news van on the corner by then, and a pudgy guy stomping around with a camera the size of a pickup's transmission. A male reporter in a flashy suit followed, taking notes as he talked to some of the neighborhood residents. "You know that guy by any chance, the reporter?"

Slade squinted into the distance. "Don't think so. Probably a young guy listening to the scanner. Trying to get a breaking story, make himself a face."

We both looked back at Chato, sprawled motionless beneath a sheet on the hot pavement. "Let's take a look at the body again, get back to the station. You get much from the kid on the bike?"

Slade shook his head, disappointed. "Nope. You started screaming as I was about to walk up on him. That fucking kid can ride a bike, I'll tell you that. He's gone until we're gone. No doubt about that."

I shrugged, headed toward Chato, our dead man. I kneeled, Slade across from me, and lifted the sheet.

His eyes shiny with interest and disgust, Slade said, "More gunshot wounds than I can count."

"More than I've ever seen."

"Hell," Slade said. "Add up all the ones I have seen—they don't come close."

I covered my mouth to cough, pinched the bridge of my nose before saying, "A job well done is a self-portrait of the person who did it."

"Meaning?"

"These motherfuckers know their business."

Slade's eyes, along with mine, lingered on Chato's body: The man's chest was ripped to shreds by bullet holes. His neck, too, seemed almost nonexistent there in the red and black and shredded skin. His torso was a mess of flesh. I imagined shredded turkey piled in a bowl—that's what Chato's flesh looked like. They left his face pristine, except for the blood he'd smeared across his own left cheek (covering his inked tears). If mommy wanted, sweet little Chato could have an open casket. I made a mental note: How considerate of his assassins. They must have known the man. And, more important, they respected him.

Slade spoke after staring for a few minutes: "I been thinking about how fast it ends, the body."

"You mean life?" Miranda's face flashed through my head.

"Not life," he said. "I mean, yeah, life. But more so the body, right? Like, the heart just stops. And it's fast when it happens. It's...biology, I guess."

"Biology?"

"Like the way cells stop multiplying. That's at the heart of this." His eyes scoured the mangled flesh below Chato's blood-smeared cheek. "It's just a bunch of cells that stop."

"It's more than biology. Shit, think of God and love and—"

"Fuck God," Slade said. "It's fucking biology, man. Run around talking faith and you're left with coal. A stocking full of coal."

"You saying you don't like Christmas?"

Slade said, "I like it fine."

"You can thank Jesus then."

Slade chuckled. "We all start from one cell. And next thing you know, we're splitting again and again until..."

I thought about Kimmie and Norton, saw their tiny baby bodies in their wet diapers. I wanted to smile, but it wouldn't come—that might've been about the body on the ground.

Slade kept talking. "A million cells, Frank. Ten million. Ten billion. It's just cells that make us stand up, walk around, take a shit, fuck for too short a time."

"Not me," I said. "I got plenty of time behind all my fucks. Never had a problem there."

He ignored me. "Yeah. We're just fucking...portfolios of cells that keep multiplying, regenerating, until one day it all stops. So goddamn sudden."

"Look, Skinny, I don't mean to interrupt this epiphany, but we need to get back and—"

Slade said, "It barely matters."

"What?"

"What we're doing. It's just chasing after dead cells."

"I think you need a drink, Skinny."

"Maybe I do."

"Let's go on over to—"

"Think about it, Frank. You're just a bunch of cells walking around, eating fucking burritos. That's all it comes down to. You and your pile of cells trying to find the next burrito."

I wanted to chuckle but couldn't with the body there beside us. "You should have been a philosopher king, Skinny. You mind keeping all this horseshit to yourself? I got a couple homicide cases to work. Last thing I need is a crazy person whispering in my ear."

Slade nodded again. He sighed and said, "Sure, Frank. I'll just keep all this to myself. We can't go around telling people murder doesn't matter."

"Right," I said.

"That wouldn't keep the peace."

"No it would not," I said. "Not at all."

Slade shut up after that—I said a prayer.

Chapter 20

On the way back to the station, Slade got a call from QB. He picked up the phone, listened while the rookie droned on about following the teenager, Turner. "Just file a report and I'll take a look," Slade said. He took a left turn too fast onto Market Street and a young hippie with matted hair and a Van Halen T-shirt had to jog across the street to avoid getting hit. QB must have insisted because Slade didn't end the call.

I peeked in the sideview mirror and saw the hippie flip us the bird. I took it as proof that world peace didn't mean a damn thing to anyone. Besides, war keeps people employed, right? Maybe Slade's death philosophy wore off on me. Or, I was still tired. I hadn't thought much about the video Jackson showed me. Riding in the car while Slade avoided potholes and smirked at QB's report jostled a fear inside me. I was one year away from a decent retirement, if I wanted it, and my indiscretion—let's call it that, okay?—meant that I put everything at risk. But then again, did I care? Miranda was gone. I never saw or heard from Norton (too important and too damn busy). And Kimmie...Kimmie spent more time being pissed at me than I did loving her.

My whole world was off balance.

But I knew that solving these cases, handing something solid to Jackson and the DA, would put me back where I needed to be. Jackson should have suspended me. I knew that. But he didn't. Because he wanted me to solve murders.

"Why can't you just put it in the fucking report," Slade was saying. He shrugged, avoided another pothole. "We don't have to meet about this, do we?" Slade glanced at me and moved his lips to one side of his face. "Okay, alright. We'll meet you at Bobo's in ten. I'll see you over there. And you're buying the drinks, rookie." Slade slid his cell back into his coat, flipped a quick U-turn at the next light. He accelerated down Market Street.

I saw the hippie's head swivel to follow as we passed him going in the opposite direction. I watched in the sideview mirror and, like I anticipated, he flipped us the bird again. "What's the kid got, Slade?"

"He said we need to meet him over at Bobo's. Got something he's keeping out of the report."

I said, "It's probably nothing. QB still has a lot to learn."

"I'm not so sure. QB's a smart cookie, Frank. Don't let his age fool you."

I shrugged, ran my palms across my thighs. My slacks were stiff with sweat and overuse. "I need some new clothes, Slade." I looked down at my tie, lifted it to my nose—pasta sauce and cheap liquor punched me in the nose, all that mixed with perpetrator sweat.

"Tell you what," Slade said, "we get through this and I'll take you downtown, a little place I know. Get you a few tailored suits, three-piece jobs that'll make you slick."

"Let's do that."

Slade took a right turn onto a street lined with windowless barrooms. It was a favorite block for the night crawlers. By that I mean the hookers and johns and lowdown pimps. This was one of those streets where we kept the problem contained. Most tourist cities do this kind of thing. You quarantine the homeless to a few square blocks, or the drug addicts, or the hookers. You let it happen, but you control where, keep it out of the brochures. The idea: If it's going to happen, all we have to do—as servants to the public—is put it out of sight. Because, you know, out of mind.

We pulled into an alley adjacent to the street, slid alongside Bobo's, and Slade shut off the engine. The bar was a cop favorite for finding confidential informants. Slade told stories about day drinking in the place. All a narc had to do was wait and, sure as shit, a junkie needing a twenty-spot would wander up, ask what you wanted to know, and who you wanted to know it about. Smart cops make decorated careers out of that sort of shit. The drug war: An ambitious cop's path to the promised land...

Inside Bobo's, QB was hunched in a booth along the far wall, past the neon-lighted bar. Me and Slade dodged the high cocktail tables in the center of the room and slid in beside QB. His eyes were red and I swore his hands shook. He lifted a beer bottle to his lips and drank in nervous sips.

"Thanks for coming, Slade. What's up, Frank?"

"What's going down, QB? You look like shit, buddy. Been drinking too much?"

QB gestured with his head at the beer. "First drink I've had since I started following that teenager. Not the last one I'm going to drink today, though."

Me and Slade traded looks—odd, to see the rookie shaken like this.

QB lifted three fingers at the bartender. A slump-backed, middle-aged woman in cutoff Levi's and a strapless white blouse placed three beers on the table. QB handed her a twenty and she left us.

"What's so fucking special you can't put it in the report, QB?" I was annoyed at wasting time on this. I always loved doing business in a bar, but this one had a cruel stink to it. I smelled day-old cold cuts and stale bread, the dead dreams of a hundred All American hookers—it got me sad.

QB looked over his shoulder, scoured the bar like his shiny eyeballs were sandpaper, and leaned across the table toward us. "Your pal Turner is a rich kid, Slade."

"What do you mean, rich kid?" Slade's surprise was modest.

As was mine.

QB said, "Turner Malcolm, stepson of a guy named Regis Decassin. He's Decassin's wife's kid, from a previous non-marriage. Out-of-wedlock, as it were." The rookie leaned back in the booth, satisfied with his fine detective work.

I said, "Who the fuck is Regis Decassin?"

Slade chuckled and said, "Frank doesn't keep up with the news, QB."

"I read the sports page." And I glanced at headlines, but I didn't say that.

Slade continued, "Decassin is a property developer, Frank. He's one of those guys that had to do with the stadium proposal. P&J Associates, I think is the firm."

QB nodded and crossed his arms. "Decassin wheels and deals, sits on a ton of committees, boards, all that shit. But he plays it really cool."

"He likes to make his money on the sly, keep it quiet." Slade drank his beer, looked at mine.

I pulled the bottle toward myself across the table, lifted it to my lips. It was slightly warm, but still good. "So, Turner's the guy's kid. We got a rich man's kid found a cartel hit down under the bay bridge. It's still not much. I mean, talking to Turner, I know he didn't chop off Castaneda's wang. Am I right?"

QB said, "You're right. But the thing is that Decassin has some other ties, down in Mexico."

"Drug ties," Slade said.

"Legitimate drug ties. All the names you see in the Mexican dailies—I checked. From what I can tell, Decassin runs a bunch of investment operations for third-party businessmen. He's got investments in a casino project in Vegas, Carson City. He's got a boat yard down in Logan Heights—"

"Right near where we found Castaneda," I said.

"—and he's been soaking up property wherever he can. Mostly, right here in the metro area."

Slade cleared his throat, watched the slump-backed waitress shuffle past us toward the bathroom. "Okay, it's no coincidence that Turner found the body, maybe because he's tied in with Decassin, runs errands or whatever. But the point here is something bigger: Decassin plays with the cartels, at least one, probably more than one, and he's digging in here in the States."

I said, "He's washing the money."

QB nodded. I'd set my beer on the table and he

leaned forward to grab my bottle. He lifted it to his lips. He gulped the entire bottle, belched. "That's right, Frank. He's washing the money. And there's something else: He's washing it through more than just gambling and property and dry-cleaning shops. Regis Decassin is a major campaign contributor to Ronald J. Applewhite."

I might spend most of my time on the sports page, but I was a murder policeman. I knew that name. "That's the guy running for the county district attorney slot."

Slade's leather jacket creaked as he tightened his biceps and leaned toward QB.

The rookie bit his bottom lip, grinned. He said, "Decassin is washing money through Applewhite's campaign. How's that for a breaking news story, Slade?"

Chapter 21

Two blocks down Broadway, around the corner from the station, there was a small bar called Goodwin's. It was a sports pub, really—somehow, they made good business playing all the Blackhawks hockey games. I never understood that, but show up on a game day and every smarmy Chi-town native banished to San Diego would be drinking beer and spitting peanut shells onto the floor. We used Goodwin's as an office away from the office. Slade had the Castaneda case file with him and I had my department-issue laptop. We were sitting at the bar, under a giant flatscreen TV barking baseball scores, and waiting for images of Chato's body—and the crime scene—to upload onto the homicide unit's private server. You could judge us for looking at this shit in public, but it wasn't hockey season. We were alone except for Raymond, the ex-Navy barman, droning on about his Chicago White Sox. Beside him, a squat, bowlegged line cook with a sideways hat and too clean white apron listened without interest.

Here we all were, punched in and on the clock. And with plenty of bourbon and beer. Not bad, unless you were dead. And looking again at the crime scene images of Castaneda's body, being dead meant torture and mutilation.

Slade flipped through the images, got frustrated. He shuffled them to the bottom of his file and pulled out his notepad, flipped to a blank sheet. "We have jack shit, Frank. Not one suspect. No leads. We don't even have a murder weapon on either of these. The best we have is the eyewitness in Chato's killing. That's all. How are we going to move forward on this?"

I checked my email again—no images yet. "Let's write down what we know, think all this shit through." I sipped from my glass of bourbon, ran my tongue over my plump lips. Like Slade, my frustration pressed against the inside of my head, but I also knew QB gave us a lead worth thinking about. All you need—those times when you've got nothing—is one small fact. "We got Applewhite at the top, okay. And that's a maybe. But it's still at the top."

Slade wrote the man's last name on top of the blank page. Below that, he wrote down Regis Decassin's name, next to that came Turner Malcolm. He put Celeste's name next to Turner's, but in parentheses. "You don't think the girl's involved, not for real?"

"Even if she's not involved, she might know something. She might know something she doesn't know she knows. That's what I'm thinking."

Slade jotted Rambo's name, too. Just above that, he listed Chato and Castaneda.

"Rambo's still around," I said, "best we know."

"That's true, but he's a street dealer, right? You and me could both see that."

"That's right," I said and waved at Raymond to come and fill my drink. "We got word out and I think

123

the street cops will bring him in."

"If he didn't bounce."

"Sure. He'll get scooped up. I can feel it. Where we have to go—I'm thinking out loud here—is to have a talk with Regis Decassin. You want the answers to these murders? I think we get the answers when we follow the money."

Slade nodded, scratched a line beneath Decassin's name. "We show up at the man's residence, say we need to talk to Turner. 'What's this about, detective?' 'Well, since you asked, Mr. Decassin…' That's how we use Turner."

Raymond poured some more liquor into my glass, looked at Slade, who was intent on his map of names. I nodded for my partner and the bartender topped off Slade's glass, too. He moved back down the bar, lifted the TV remote and raised the volume. More baseball—in-depth analysis from your resident hall-of-famer.

"And we get in there and, somehow, we chat about all the man's investments, his dealings. We start to talk about the money, see where it comes from."

I said, "I think you just pretend to admire Decassin. Make it seem like we see him as a big city type, Mr. Fucking Important. We're not going for some kind of admission."

"Right, we want his trust," Slade said. "We want him to think we're stupid." Slade chuckled. "Maybe we are."

I thought about how the Jacoby case might tie in and groaned.

"What is it?" Slade circled Decassin's name now, drew an arrow to Applewhite's entry.

"I just remembered I forgot to ask Richie and Donovan about the Jacoby case, how it got taken from them. If Decassin is tied to Jacoby through business dealings, I see no reason why we don't bring that up with him. Give him our regards, you know? Man's business partner gets put down, I imagine he feels some way about it."

Slade licked his lips, sipped from his glass. He leaned back in his chair and crossed his arms. "That's true and, fuck, maybe Richie and Donovan know something about Decassin."

I left Slade at the bar and stepped outside to give Donovan a call. Me and him went back a few years. I worked a few cases with him when I first joined homicide. I listened to the rushing, ceaseless traffic pass on Broadway, found Donovan's last name in my phone, and dialed his number. He picked up after three rings.

"This is Detective Donovan Dillahunt."

"Hey, Donovan: It's Frank."

"Frank Pinson. No shit? What's going on, partner?"

"Ah, caught two bodies this weekend. I'm running around a house of mirrors, buddy."

"Man, I picked a good time for cashing in on vacation days. I heard about the one under the bridge. You got another one?"

I paced back and forth on the sidewalk, rubbed sweat off the back of my neck. "Yeah. It's related. Neighborhood thing in the hood. Looks like a cartel hit. What I'm calling about, though, is the Jacoby case."

Donovan whistled. "Shit, they found the Jacobys out near Jacumba. It's looking like the feds screwed the pooch, missed something. Can't say I didn't see that coming."

I said, "Me and Slade found the Jacobys, Donovan.

After a tip from the kid who ran across Castaneda's body." I waited for Donovan's silent surprise to end. A city bus hummed past me followed by a cyclist and two motorcycles. A line of cars stopped at the nearest streetlight. On the sidewalk, a group of men with briefcases brushed by me, none of them talking to each other.

"You're shitting me—that was you two? You didn't call me about it." His anger showed through in his pronouns. "Why the fuck didn't you call me?"

"We thought it was bullshit, Don. Went out there because that was what the kid who found our body gave us—"

"I'm gone two weeks and I don't exist, huh?"

"I should have called," I said.

"No shit, Frank."

"Look, Don, you remember why it was the feds swiped the case from you? And who it was?"

He grunted and cleared his throat. "You're an asshole, Pinson." He was pissed, but he kept talking. "Jackson served it up, as I remember. We fought about it for a minute, but then I thought, 'Who gives a shit? Might as well let the feds take the red ball.' You know how that is."

"You have a contact over there? Who took the case?" I listened to the dead sound of Donovan thinking with his booze-addled brain.

"Fuck me, man. It's probably written down somewhere."

"Yeah," I said. "I guess I'll do some digging and—"

"That's right. I remember. It was Dames, Xander Dames. Some special fucking agent of something or the other. Gave me a call and demanded I give him everything I had. Didn't even want to meet for a beer. Fucking feds, Frank."

"Xander Dames? You're sure?"

"That's right."

"And you ever run across a name in your investigation, man by the name of Regis Decassin?"

"We sure did," Donovan said. "Decassin was in business with Jacoby. They sat on some board or some such thing together. Rich guy stuff...I think it was—"

"P&J Associates?" I said.

"You got it. We never talked to Decassin—he was out of the country on business. The feds took the case before I ever got to meet the man. It was just me chasing loose ends, though. Decassin was out of the country even when the Jacoby family went missing."

I thought for a second and asked a question I knew Donovan didn't have the answer for. But then again, sometimes you get a nice surprise in the mystery business. "We've been looking at this Jacoby thing being tied in with the Castaneda murder. You know what the P stands for in P&J?"

Donovan laughed, surprised. "That's a funny question, but I do know what it stands for—it's not a name. That's what's funny. I think this came from Decassin's secretary, but it stands for a Spanish word..." He popped his tongue against his cheek a few times and said: "Pie-say-no, maybe?"

I got a funny feeling in my throat and my run-of-the-mill Spanish shot across my lips. "You trying to say...Paisano?"

"That's it. Pie-say-no and Jacoby Associates. I wrote it down—all this shit is in the case file."

"Thanks, Don. I'll check it out. Thanks for answering my call."

"Frank, do me a fucking favor?"

"What's that?"

"You call and let me know the next time you find one of my fucking bodies."

As I was about to walk back into Goodwin's, a young man with wet brown hair wearing an ironed black polo shirt brushed past me. He was slightly shorter than me, but well-built and with a determined look on his face. What caught my eye was the gold pendant dangling from a gold chain around his neck—Santa Muerte. It looked a lot like the pendant Chato wore when we interviewed him, though his was attached to rosary beads. The necklace was still on Chato's neck when we inspected his body, the pendant somehow untouched by all the gunfire and blood. I sniffed the young man's cheap cologne—it trailed behind him through the car exhaust and fast-food smells—and stopped myself. I decided I needed to know more about Lady Death, as popular as she seemed to be in these intertwined brutal murders. I whirled to follow the young man. I thought I might tap him on the shoulder, ask some general questions about Lady Death. But instead I fell back, hovered behind him as he made a quick right through a crowd of business men swinging briefcases, and hurried down an alleyway.

The alley was dark and cool, shaded from the sun by two buildings. A chain hotel stretched high above me on one side and an apartment building towered on the other. I looked up and saw the apartment building still had one of those ancient fire escapes, a metal stairway that zigzagged from floor to floor. I hunched next to the old-style brickwork of the building and watched the young man enter a doorway at the alley's far end. The metallic crunch of machines came from the doorway when he opened it, collapsed into silence as the door closed.

I jogged down the alley, sidestepped two stagnant puddles of green water and weaved between three trash dumpsters. The alley looked like it served as the back entry for a series of businesses on the avenue, the food stalls and barbershop below the apartment building and, on the hotel side, the hotel laundry and kitchen. When I reached the young man's doorway, I found I was correct—it was the hotel laundry room.

When I yanked the door open, a blast of heat smacked me in the face and I almost sneezed at the pungent odor of industrial grade cleaners—a smell like pine mixed with sulfur and soap and warm water. The metallic noise churned in my ears. I walked in and began to sweat beneath my long-sleeve dress shirt. A round woman with thick glasses and red hair piled high in a bun waved at me. She was stuffing hotel room sheets into a commercial-grade washing machine. I swore it looked like a huge silver space shuttle. I waved and slid past her, watched for the black fabric of the young man's polo shirt.

I moved slowly against a thick, flapping white wall of dangling hotel robes. I pushed a robe aside, stepped through, saw the young man moving between a long row of wheeled carts piled high with beige, soiled towels. I shouted after him and he stopped. As soon as my hand went beneath my suit coat and reappeared with my badge, the young man took off. Of course, I thought, he's got a warrant or something and here I am trying to ask the kid about his superstition. I sprinted to cut him off from the exit. He was circling back, trying to get to the same door where we both entered the laundry room. He dodged behind a row of drying machines and I angled toward the other side. I heard the woman shout as I rammed into him. We both tumbled, a clumsy symphony of limbs and grunts and pained expressions, and skidded across the polished concrete floor. He was struggling as we flew, reminded me of a puppy when you try to hug it as tight as you can. We both smacked our heads against the stainless-steel base of another odd laundry machine and there was a brief pause. I said, "It's okay. I don't care about your trouble."

He struggled harder, found a way to escape my grip. After a few exchanged holds, he was on top of me with a fist in my face. My throat felt small, constricted, cut off from the vault of air in my belly. His strength was wiry, deceptive. Strength gained from hard labor and sacrifice. You know that muscle when it's used against you—there's no mistaking where it comes from, how it got there. His left hand gripped my neck and the calluses on his palm scraped my skin. An image of Slade hunched over the bar at Goodwin's, likely checking the time on his cell, flashed through my mind. Slade saying to himself, "Where the hell is Frank?" as I was about to get my face decorated by a scrappy hotel worker. I saw the young man's fist clench tight, his bicep scrunch into a hard ball, and I screamed: "Santa Muerte! Santa Muerte! Santa Muerte!"

His eyes widened, centered on my moving lips.

The Santa Muerte pendant dangled in front of me, swung from left to right, its gold color glinting in the halogen light. I reached out with a free hand, closed my fingers around it. "Santa Muerte," I said. "La Bonita. The White Lady."

The young man's fist stayed right where it was.

Ricky held the pendant while he talked to me and, as he did, I began to think of it more like a charm than a pendant. It was a cultural object with magic inside it. I saw that in Ricky's eyes, and I began to feel it inside me. We stood outside in the dark, cool alley. Ricky placed one foot flat against the building, leaned sideways on the other. He wore a semi-smile while he spoke. And I liked him. Knowing he bested me in our scuffle made me like him more.

"You're lucky I didn't hit you, Detective. Maybe I would have messed up your face."

I shook my head, played with my tie. I patted the silver handcuffs holstered on my belt. "Shoot, Ricky. You hit me and I would have taken you to jail before the blood dried on my lips. You're a strong cookie, huh?"

Ricky looked down the alley, didn't seem to acknowledge the compliment. "What you want to know about the lady, Detective? You trying to convert or something?"

I said, "From what?"

Ricky laughed and said, "You got Catholic written all over you."

"How's that?"

"I heard all cops are Catholic," Ricky said. "That's how those old movies do it."

"All the good cops are Catholic," I said. "Even the

movies get shit right once in a while." I told him I wanted to know about Santa Muerte, how he came to believe in her. I wanted to know what she was to him, how it all worked. "I know it takes some rituals from Catholicism, okay? I'm not some hardcore bastard who gives two shits about that. Let me be clear: I'm looking into some murders and it seems like the lady there—" I pointed at his hand wrapped around the charm. "—is some part of the whole thing."

He said, "It's because the White Lady deals in vengeance."

"What's that mean?"

"You want some revenge, you just ask her. She can give it to you."

I watched him with interest. He was well-groomed, but still had a roughness about him. I got the sense he had trouble sleeping. His eyes were dark and set back far in his head. His fingernails were cut short, but slim moons of dirt showed beneath them. "Where you do the praying around here, Ricky? They have a shrine around here?" I thought again about the shrines in the neighborhood where Chato met God (or his White Lady). I wondered who asked for vengeance against Chato, whether Santa Muerte made choices between people. That's the problem with believing all sorts of shit you can't see—it's full of paradox and senseless logic. As a Catholic and a murder detective, I knew paradox and senseless logic like I knew the penal code. But there I went thinking too hard again.

Ricky watched me, too. I saw the thoughts turning in his head, behind those see-it-all eyes. Why should I let you in? Who do you think you are? Go fuck yourself, Detective.

"Maybe she doesn't want you to see her. You think about that?" His eyes fell to the pavement and he shifted against the wall, leaned so it looked like he was holding up the entire building.

"You work here?"

He nodded and said, "In the laundry."

"You like it?"

"Why, you going to get me something better?"

I shook my head. "You don't need me for anything, Ricky—I know that."

"What's the point of your question?"

"I'm trying to get to know you, my fellow citizen. Shit, I'm just being friendly. Is something wrong with that? You're the one who wanted to hit me."

"And you want me to show you my saint. I'm talking to you and looking at you, but I'm thinking you don't see. You don't believe."

"What's to see, Ricky? I'm trying to get to know her. I want to believe, man."

"Maybe you say you do, but it's easy to talk. Like everybody, all the Catholics, maybe you're going to call me a witch, say I'm perverted. You're going to burn down my church, call it a cult." He dropped his hand from the Santa Muerte charm and it bounced into his chest.

"I'm a detective, Ricky. The things I do are for families, for people to know the truth. I'm out here trying to find a way for death to make sense. That's all I am, all I'm doing."

He shrugged and said, "You get a curse if you laugh at her."

"There's nothing funny about the two dead men I've seen the past few days," I said. But my mind flashed on the desert and the Jacoby girl's dead hand, how it jutted from the sand like she was reaching for me from her shallow grave. "Death is my work, and it's nothing to laugh about. Or to mock. I hope you know that."

"What do you want with the White Lady then?"

I said, "I'm trying for justice, Ricky. That's why I want to know. I'm doing what's right."

Ricky nodded, pushed himself away from the wall. He balanced atop one foot, took a long slow step, and turned to fully face me. Behind him, the dark alley framed his face and his eyes seemed brighter somehow, like I flipped a power switch in his head. He said, "You want to go to church, Detective? I have some time before work—let's go."

"Where's it at? I need to let my partner know."

Ricky was already past me and halfway down the alley, headed toward the busy street. He called out to me in an eerie voice, "It's not far, Detective. You'll be home in no time."

Chapter 22

It was still hot. The afternoon had worn on in the way they tend to do. As I walked with Ricky east on Broadway, we passed a group of Somali cab drivers sipping coffee outside a liquor store, dodged a bus as it pulled to a stop for a group of uniformed high school students, and waded through the crowd of retail and office workers headed toward the nearest trolley stop. The sun hit our backs and I felt sweat pool in the center of my back and run down to my waistband. It was a welcome change when Ricky headed south on a side street. The street ran alongside a tow yard and the rear loading dock of a Salvation Army storefront. On the opposite side of the street, I noted the 4500 block addresses of a tailor, a tire shop, and two or three bars I'd never frequented. Ricky moved fast and my breathing quickened as he hustled along the sidewalk. He told me he needed to clock in at the hotel by four—we had almost thirty minutes. I imagined Slade could wait that long for me to show up at Goodwin's. If not, it wasn't the end of the world. He'd chew me out, but I could take care of myself. Slade knew that.

Ricky stopped after we passed the Salvation Army. I

noted a few frayed couches dumped in the lot, numerous piles of old clothes and, in one large area, a jumble of particle board and pine—desks and dressers and random armoires.

We turned right and walked through an empty parking lot toward a small white building with gang writing scrawled on one side. Above the building, the cityscape loomed like the open mouth of a dog. The entrance had a keypad, like what you'd see at fast food restaurants: A vertical row of silver buttons had to be pressed in the right order, otherwise the door wouldn't unlock. Ricky punched the buttons—I tried to memorize the pattern, but he moved in front of me and I wasn't sure I got it—and the door swung open into cool dark air.

Inside, I smelled incense and sulfur. A small radio played Mariachi music somewhere out of sight. Ricky moved forward and crossed through a hallway, turned right into a doorless and windowless room. There were candles lit at the front of the room—I counted ten rows of foldable steel chairs, maybe fifteen to a row. The candles flanked a likeness of Santa Muerte, and I shivered when I took in the sight: It was a reclining skeleton with a dark hooded cape drawn over it, a reaper's blade propped between its bony legs. The skeleton was propped up on what looked like a throne, all plush red fabric and golden armrests. The candlelight hit the bones with delicate splashes of fiery illumination. The scene appeared manufactured, like an amusement park ride, but my mouth dried when I saw it and my groin pulled up into my swollen belly. I swear the skeleton's eyes shined and I blinked hard to clear my vision. Tears welled in my eyes and I didn't understand what was happening to me. I followed Ricky through the chairs and the incense smell got stronger while the sulfur vanished. We stopped a few feet from the figure and I reached up to wipe my cheek—my right hand came away wet and it surprised me. The yellow candle-light made the skeleton seem to twist and shake in front of me. The light flitted through the visible white bones and reflected off the dark cape.

Beside me, Ricky kneeled and began to mumble. He closed one hand over the gold charm around his neck, and he swayed to the rhythm of his own voice.

I didn't know what to do. After some hesitation, I wiped my tears across my chest and kneeled beside Ricky. I crossed myself without thinking. I bowed my head. I heard Ricky's voice, but the words were faint, a selection of Spanish I didn't know well enough to pick out at his subdued volume. He sniffed twice and I turned to see that he, too, was crying. I reached up and wiped more tears from my cheeks. I was unsettled. My groin pulled up higher into my belly and my throat constricted. I had the overwhelming urge to weep. It was a feeling I knew well from the previous six months, but one I'd never allowed to grip me. I shoved it back down inside, buried it in the deepest parts of my being. But somehow being there in front of Santa Muerte, the feeling seemed too powerful to suppress.

I heard a sob and realized it came from my own mouth.

I looked into the skeleton's eyes. Shiny and deep, like pools of black water. I sobbed again and Ricky's voice beside me went silent. The heat from the flickering candles warmed my face. Another sob. I closed my eyes. For a moment, I saw only blackness and felt the warm candlelight against my closed eyelids. But the darkness gave way to a shimmer. I tried to see through it, with my eyes closed, and it began to wave. It was like moving through water. From a great distance, I heard more sobbing. My body lightened, lifted. I kept moving through the water and went deeper, deeper, deeper. Until the candlelight didn't feel warm on my face. Until I shivered and shook. Goosebumps erupted on the back of my neck and I squinted without squinting—I tried to see into the cold black waters.

That's when I realized I wasn't descending, but rather the water was flowing over me, rising toward me, into me, closing all around me. I couldn't breathe, but the water cleared, grew thin. I felt warm all over and a face appeared in front of me—it was my wife. It was Miranda. Her lips bloated, purple with blood. And her hazel eyes had a dead look to them—an anti-shine that made me think of matte finish spray paint. She's floating, I thought.

My God, Miranda's floating.

But my body tightened. Transformed from warm to hot. Sweat ran across my face and neck and shoulders. It dripped onto the backs of my hands, pooled on my upper lip.

Kneeling there in front of Santa Muerte, with my eyes still squeezed shut, I watched Miranda's bloated face slip beneath a sheen of blackish water, grow faint, sink into the sea of my mind.

And she was gone.

Chapter 23

I woke up with my face planted into cold dirty cement, my mouth dry and sticky. I shifted to my knees. The candles still burned, though shorter and with smaller flames. And she was there, Santa Muerte. I stared at her for a minute before hearing shoes scuff the carpet behind me. I turned to see a short Mexican woman in a slim, dark-colored pantsuit. She was a thin woman, but the way she moved—she came toward me in a few short steps—spoke of strength and surety. She lowered a hand and I took it, let her yank me—a near-fat man—to my feet. I towered over the woman, but I felt small. I'd felt that way around other men, sure, but never with a woman.

She glared at me and smirked. "You fell asleep beside our White Lady, the White Sister."

"I think…" I ran my tongue up and down the sides of my mouth. It was like scraping stone with sandpaper. "I think I passed out. Maybe I—"

"You let the lady do her work." She moved past me to lower her head beside the skeletal figure.

I turned and watched. "Are you one of her followers?"

Without looking at me, the woman said, "We don't follow her. She gives us gifts, answers our prayers. If you have something you need, the lady will listen to you. In turn, we listen to ourselves. This is all she wants from us."

I knew it sounded odd, slightly mystical and un-founded. But I remembered that feeling of black water moving into me, the image of Miranda surfacing, and I believed the woman. Not fully. Not in the sense that I worshipped Santa Muerte, but in the sense that—in the woman's own mind—she was giving me the truth. I listened to her and I heard the truth. I'd heard so many lies in my life. I knew the timbre of lies, the occult melody of murder and denial. This woman didn't speak that way—the criminal way.

I said, "Has she done anything for you?"

She lifted her bowed head, stared into the skeleton's eyes. "She killed my husband. I thank her every day for that. And I know it was the work of vengeance, because vengeance is an answered prayer." She turned and held out her hand. "I'm Vera. I'm caretaker for this place."

I shook her hand. I looked around at the room again—a church, really—and turned back to Vera with confusion. "Is this a...church? A shrine?"

"We started here because nobody will have us." She motioned toward the skeleton. "They fear the lady and, maybe more, they fear the church."

"You mean—"

"Catholics." She half-smiled. "Like you, mister..."

"Pinson," I said. "Frank Pinson."

"Police?"

"I am, but I'm not here for that, to give you any trouble."

She walked past me through the rows of chairs, sat down in one near the back of the room. The metal creaked under her slight weight. "If Ricky brings you here, I cannot deny you. My role is to bring people to Her, to let them pray, to have those prayers answered."

I said, "Like a priest."

"I'm not a priest, Mr. Pinson. I'm a caretaker. That's all."

I moved through the chairs. My legs were weak and I was thirsty. In the back of my mind, I worried about Slade, what I'd tell him. I stopped in front of Vera and cleared my throat. "I'm a detective here in the city and—"

"I can see that."

"I'm investigating two murders. Each victim was connected to this," I said motioning at the shrine. "To Santa Muerte. One had a tattoo and the other carried a rosary—" I caught myself and said, "A charm around his neck. They were both gangsters, and we think—"

"Narcos," she said. "Traffickers."

"That's correct."

She straightened in her seat, brushed off her pantsuit. "I know about the murders, but it's not what you think, Detective. It runs deeper than you imagine." She looked past me toward the figure at the front of the room, the skeleton bathed in candlelight and prayer. "Santa Muerte is with you, Detective. She's angry. Like you. She's grieving. Like you."

"What do you mean by that?"

"I mean that the lady is grieving. She's lost something. And haven't you?"

The warm, swallowed-up feeling I had beside Santa Muerte faded, and I got angry. It happened in an instant. "What do you know about what I've lost?"

Vera shook her head, stood, walked away from me.

She grabbed a vacuum-broom leaning against a wall and began running it across the thin carpet. "I don't know anything," she said. "But Santa Muerte knows everything. Some say she is the Saint of Narcos. But sometimes we forget, even people who do bad things need a saint. Isn't that true?"

I turned and studied the figure again. Anger spread through my body like a rising, uncontrollable fever. I wasn't mad at Vera or Saint Death. No, I couldn't be. I was mad instead at the world for being what it was. I was mad at the nonsense of death, at the futility of murder and its cruel punishments. I was mad at being alive while my wife slept in a coffin. And I was angry at my faith for talking saviors and disciples and promises of heaven. In that moment, staring at Saint Death, I didn't believe a damn word of what I'd learned. Fuck Sunday school, I thought, my wife is dead. And I wanted to get back at something or somebody for that—I wanted vengeance, and I didn't give one fat shit where or who I got it from. I left the Santa Muerte shrine with that feeling raging in my head and through my whole body.

I still carry that feeling, but vengeance is no savior. I know that now. But I didn't know it then and—this, I promise you—I wouldn't know it for a long, long while.

I stumbled back to Goodwin's and wasn't surprised to find Slade long gone. I ordered a drink and sat there cursing God for a good half hour. I wanted to spend the night drinking and fuming and feeling sorry for myself and the dead. But I knew Jackson needed me and Slade to solve the Castaneda murders. And I knew Slade—

whether he admitted it or not—was worried about me. Slade was a worrier, and I gave him cause to worry. An imperfectly perfect partnership, I thought.

And the Castanedas were dead. As bad as they were, whatever they did, the dead needed me. I used my cell to call Slade from the bar. When he answered, I said, "I was chasing down a lead. Know that before you cuss me out."

Slade sighed. I knew he was posted up at his desk digging through phone records, or sifting through campaign funding documents, or whatever the hell else a responsible detective did. "I bet you were, Frank. You're always chasing down something."

"I talked to Donovan. They knew about Decassin, but he had an alibi for when the Jacobys went missing. Case got taken by our pal Xander Dames, one and the same, and the business dealings between Jacoby and Decassin were known to the detectives, to the feds…Hell, to everybody."

"Except for me and you," Slade said.

"We know now. I'm thinking that Dames guy, and his partner, Miss what's-her-face—"

"Atkins. Tracy Atkins."

"That's it. I'm betting the two of them are protecting somebody. Maybe Applewhite. Or someone close to him. That makes sense to me. If Decassin is a big donor to Applewhite's campaign, if they were gearing up for a DA run, the Jacobys disappearing would kill it."

I heard Slade grunt and scratch his chin. "That could be. So, the agents quash the inquiry into Jacobys' business dealings. Which would lead to Applewhite, one way or another, and the man gets elected. Except for one fucking thing, right?"

"Castaneda gets got," I said. "And then me and you find the Jacoby family." Neither of us spoke for some time and I watched the television above the bar. One of those mixed martial arts fights was playing and a young kid with tribal tattoos and a soul patch was pummeling a redneck from Tuscaloosa. He punched him hard in the face until the redneck tapped out. The referee jumped in and pulled the winner to the corner of the cage. "And now," I said, "me and you are caught in the middle of some political shitstorm because if we bring this to Jackson—"

"We're not bringing shit to Jackson until we use our handcuffs."

"Okay," I said. "What do you want to do then?"

Slade sighed again and breathed hard through the phone. "I'm about to look into the campaign donations now. Let's make sure we've got that as legit. And then, if it comes out true, I think we have a nice civil conversation with Decassin."

"And when he tells us to fuck off?"

Slade sucked air through his teeth. "We threaten to go to the press. I know a reporter who could really use a big break. This would be a great fucking story."

My yellow piss ran in a circle around the porcelain urinal, pooled in the silver drain, and seeped into the pipes below the city. I zipped up, flushed the urinal and moved to the bathroom sink. Goodwin's was plastered with stickers declaring Chicago sports teams God's gift to Earth. I pinched a Blackhawks sticker between thumb and forefinger, ripped it off the wall. I crumpled it up and tossed it into the trash can. I had to get back to the office and help Slade dig through campaign donation records, but I drank a few beers to relax. I might not be walking straight when I got to the station, but I'd be breathing easier. I flipped on the hot water, started to soap my hands. When I heard the bathroom door whoosh open, I looked in the mirror. For a moment there was only a shadow there. It lingered for a second, let the door whoosh closed, and moved forward. Probably some drunk taking a piss, I thought. I focused on washing my hands and, for some reason, I couldn't get Miranda's face off my mind. I kept seeing those bloated lips from my experience with Santa Muerte. I closed my eyes, squeezed. But I opened them when I felt a presence behind me. You know that feeling—a heaviness behind you, like your shadow gained weight. In the mirror's reflection I saw a man much shorter than me. He had a bruised face and one side of his head looked plump, like a ripe fruit ballooned with a day's heat.

It was Johnny. And he was smiling.

I noticed half his teeth were black with blood.

He said, "How do you do, Detective Pinson? Odd to see you two evenings in a row, isn't it?"

"You the one who sent that fucking video?"

Johnny didn't answer. Instead, he reached into his coat and pulled out some brass knuckles. He slipped them over his right hand. Before I could turn around or duck away, Johnny's arm swung upwards and around in a loping-hooking punch that connected with the right side of my face.

Blood flew from my mouth and splattered the mirror. I fell to my knees and couldn't block or avoid the second punch. Of course, I saw nothing because I was already deep into the recesses of unconsciousness.

Chapter 24

When I stumbled into the station, Slade had his coat off, his sleeves rolled to his biceps, and he was sifting through a stack of papers with yellow highlighting. My head throbbed like a beating heart and I had blood caked on one side of my face—it stuck to my right ear and cheek, seeped from my gums. I drank what blood I could, but some of it dripped over my bottom lip. "Sorry it took me so long," I said and sank into my chair beside Slade. I stared at the ceiling.

He didn't look at me right away. That took a few seconds.

"You know, Frank. I'm getting sick of covering for your ass. Jackson was down my throat about where the fuck you were and I had to lie to him. Again. If this shit keeps happening, I swear to you I'm going to—"

"I got tied up, Skinny."

He dropped the sheaf of papers in his hand, swiveled in his chair. "Oh, shit. What the fuck happened to you, Frank?"

Slade yanked at my chin before I flinched.

I groaned.

"You need a paramedic, Frank."

"Fuck that, Skinny. I'm fine. Just give me an aspirin or three." I pulled away from him. My chair rolled back into the empty office's center. "Does anybody else work cases in this fucked up city? Where is everybody?"

Slade opened a drawer in his desk and started digging through it. He came out with a bottle of pills and tossed it to me. "Jackson and everybody else went up to the casino to watch the fight."

I twisted the pill bottle's top, yanked it off. I poured a handful of the white pills into my mouth, crunched them into powder. "And they're clocked in? What the fuck?"

"Because you're such a fucking saint?" Slade looked at me without pity. "Way I see it, I'm the only one around here earning my pay. Maybe I should take that shit to the press. I'm wondering if you're going to give me your story, Frank." He pointed at my face.

"After I got back to Goodwin's, I got clocked in the bathroom."

"What for, Frank?"

"The fuck if I know. I didn't even see the guy."

Slade sat there with calm, sad eyes. He crossed his arms. "Fine, Frank. Whatever you say. How about before that? You ran off somewhere, right? Or was that just me lost in my own fucking time warp? And don't treat me like a rookie, Frank. I'm really sick of covering—"

"I found a place where they worship the Death Saint. I'm on the street talking to Donovan and I see a kid walk by with that same pendant around his neck, the one Chato wore. I stopped him and asked about it." I recounted following Ricky downtown and how he showed me the shrine, but I left out the part about praying with him and, most important, all the weird shit about me crying and seeing Miranda's face. I figured Slade didn't need to know that.

Nobody did but me. It was personal.

"You get anything good from your little pilgrimage?"

If you only knew, I thought. But instead I said, "Met a lady who runs the joint. Word's already out about the Castaneda brothers taking the long goodbye. But not much more than that. I think Decassin's our big break. We need to chat with the guy."

Slade turned back to the papers on his desk and lifted one. "I highlighted all the donations to Applewhite's campaign that didn't come from individuals or easily identifiable organizations. There's lots of shit that looks weird, but the bigger deal is this." Slade tapped his keyboard and the computer screen lit up. A simple website with a telling title: "Political Action Committee to Elect Ronald Applewhite." The logo was the acronym—PACERA—in red, white, and blue block letters. "Applewhite," Slade said, "has himself a PAC. And they've done a decent job. By that I mean they've done one hell of a job on the money front."

"You're telling me Decassin runs the PAC?"

Slade shrugged and crossed his arms again. He squinted at me in the way people with graduate degrees often squint at fat men. "No telling who really runs the PAC, but I'd bet my last paycheck it was Decassin." He smirked and turned his head to study the computer screen. "Politics, man—it always gets somebody killed."

Slade would know. I nodded and leaned my head to one side. My cheek felt swollen and the right side of my mouth ached. It was getting late and I began to think that a few hours' sleep would do me well. Ice pack, bourbon, and a few sleeping pills—all those goodies called my name. But I knew Slade far too well. "Let me guess," I said, "you want to run out and surprise Decassin tonight. See how well he thinks in his pajama bottoms."

"Shit," Slade said, "you and me both know a murder investigation never stops."

I rolled my eyes. Again, my fucking partner was right. I took daily inventory: First, there was a brutality allegation caught on camera. Second, we had the other Castaneda body. We had the cowboy snapping my picture at the crime scene. We had QB putting us on Decassin, and maybe Applewhite. And we had Donovan's information coupled with the political action committee. I put the Santa Muerte shrine and my spiritual experience—should I call it that?—in another list altogether. Maybe it was on the same list with Johnny clobbering me over at Goodwin's. Fuck it, I thought, might as well visit Decassin and complete the order. I said, "It's up north, right? You can drive."

"We need to wash that blood off your face first. I'll drive, but while I do, you're going to come clean. I want you to tell me who took brass knuckles to your head. And why."

"It's personal, Skinny."

"Good," he said. "That means you're fucking it up, and you need my help."

Fucking lawyers, I thought. They think they're so goddamn righteous.

Chapter 25

On the drive north, I told Skinny about the video of me pummeling Johnny.

He put my new injuries together with that story and said, "So, you somehow went and made a man of the cloth your number one enemy." The car's engine groaned as Slade powered into the fast lane. "Went and got yourself a starring role in a viral video. That's smart, Frank."

"I don't think I'd call him a man of the cloth."

Slade tilted his head from one shoulder to the other. "Well, he works at a church, but the man meets you and now he's cracking skulls with brass knuckles. What do you say to that, Frank? Now me and Jackson are up to our asses in your shit. Same as always."

"You don't know everything, Skinny."

Slade frowned at me, swung his pesky peepers back to the dark highway. He shifted lanes, crossed to an exit. As he applied the brakes, he said, "That's the biggest problem here, partner. We keep walking around, acting like we're in this thing together. Meantime, you got some shit I need to know about. And it's some real shit, too. The kind that can get me hurt and—"

"You weren't there."

"But I could have been," Slade said. "And I'll be fucked sideways if I'm going to let some youth pastor get the drop on my partner. And that's what I mean when I say that you—"

"Miranda slept with the man," I said. "It happened a few weeks before she..." I paused and tasted the words on my tongue. Like swishing year-old coffee in my mouth. "Before she jumped. Before she killed herself."

The way Slade's shoulders slumped, I felt bad for telling him. There are personal things grown men shouldn't discuss. And for me to tell Slade, after all the shit I've dealt with, and with how he remembered Miranda, that she cheated on me—I knew it meant a quiet rage inside him.

There was a stop sign where the exit ramp met the road to Decassin's neighborhood and Slade stopped the car. He squeezed the steering wheel for a minute, a half-assed attempt to control himself. He looked both ways down the empty road, but didn't make the right hand turn the voice coming from his cell insisted he make. He shook his head in violent denial. "You can't fucking tell me that Miranda cheated on you, Frank. There's no way you can tell me that."

"I just did tell you that, Skinny. Didn't want to, but I did."

"That woman. She..." He trailed off, whistled a low tone.

"Miranda was a fucking saint," I said.

"God, I loved her," he said.

"Yeah, me too. You probably shouldn't blame Miranda. I mean, hell, you know how much I work. And it's not like I made much effort to keep shit together.

151

Any effort. None at all." I cleared my throat and fought back some sobs. The pain in my head flared now and then, like a drone soaring back and forth overhead. "I'm a bad husband. Or, shit, I was a bad husband."

"I'll tell you what, Frank. Some shit I do not understand."

He made the right turn and got the car up to the forty-five limit. The road weaved through tall stands of mesquite trees and, farther on, a surprising wealth of pines. We stopped after about two miles, when the road ran into a guarded entrance, and Slade punched off his GPS application. The cell disappeared into his coat. We were about ten feet in front of the guardhouse. "I wish you would have told me, Frank. I'm no shrink, but it's not like—"

"It's one of those things. It's embarrassing. For me it is."

Slade didn't respond. He pulled next to the guardhouse and rolled down his window. A chubby teen in khaki pants and a wrinkled beige polo shirt opened a door and leaned into the window. When I saw his face, I realized the chubby guard wasn't a teenager, but more likely in his mid-twenties. He had the vague facial expressions of a failed actor, and a nose that belonged in a paper bag.

I said, "We want to see Regis Decassin."

The chubby guard said, "Did Mr. Decassin call ahead about you?"

Slade and me produced our badges at the same time. The shields glinted in the orange-ish light cast by the guardhouse lamppost. "We're detectives," I said, "and we just need to chat with Mr. Decassin. I appreciate how thorough you are, but we're just going to be—"

"It doesn't matter if you're the president of these United States. Truth is, I'm supposed to vet everyone who comes in here. No exceptions. They got me on camera," the guard tilted his head behind our car, "and I can get fired if I don't follow procedure."

I thought I smelled potato chips and ranch dip on the guard's breath. Slade was leaning back in his seat, as if trying to avoid a bee buzzing near his chin. He smelled it too.

"Look, son—"

"I'm not your son," the guard said rolling his eyes.

"That's true," I said, "but you're sure as shit somebody's son. And if you don't open that fucking gate, you're going to be somebody's bitch." It felt good to let my anger run out of me. I felt like an ice cube thawing on a warm sidewalk. "I wonder if you know how much shit I can shovel onto a fat rent-a-cop in too short khakis?"

The guard smirked and said, "I don't suppose you know the password, do you?"

"Open sesame?" Slade grinned at his own joke.

The guard backed away from the car. "Let me phone Mr. Decassin. I'll let you know, sirs."

"Detectives," I said.

The guard entered his station and, through the tinted windows, I saw him pick up a phone and dial a number. I looked at Slade and couldn't contain my disappointment. "Open sesame? That's all you got for an opening like that?"

"I didn't think it was too bad. Doesn't compare to 'I'm going to make you somebody's bitch.'"

"A tad cliché, huh?"

Slade shrugged. "You're getting fed up with all the run around in this case. Shit, in both these cases. I can see that and I respect it. All I want is for you to keep it legal, know what I mean?"

I did know what Slade meant, but I didn't give two fat shits. I had a headache. Some chubby rent-a-cop was giving me backtalk, and I wanted a break in the two murders I needed to solve by Monday. "Yeah, Slade," I said. "I get it—no funny stuff around Detective Slade Ryerson. Not on his watch. I'm just wondering, with all your fucking wisdom and riches, what the hell we're going to do about the video that shows me punching a man of the cloth into dark submission?"

Slowly, the gate swung upward and cleared our path.

Slade shifted the car into drive, slid forward while his window closed on the approaching guard. As we passed through the open gate, Slade turned to me and said, "I don't know, Frank. Might be you have to face a fact: Sometimes you can be a real asshole."

"And you're perfect?"

"Detective Ryerson is spick and span, my man. I'm clean as a bobby pin. Spick and fucking span."

The housing development—country club, really—was comprised of wide streets named for valuable jewels. Ruby Place. Diamond Circle. Sapphire Drive. We took Amethyst Lane. It ran through manicured lawns and well-tended flower beds. Each yard flanked a large garage with a golf cart bay and, to the left or right, a mission-inspired home. Built with red tile roofs and splashed with beige desert colors. Glass block featured prominently on one side or another. Large windows looked out on low-walled courtyards. As Slade steered along the rolling street, we searched for Decassin's address. I thought about how we were many dimensions removed from the neighborhood where Chato bit his bullets, and from where the Santa Muerte shrine called to me. Gated communities, I thought, are the most recent manifestation of royalty.

"How much you think these places go for, Frank?"

I sighed and said, "You're looking at a million dollars."

"Just to play golf in the morning, huh?"

"Shit," I said. "You got to pay for that, too. Club fees, partner."

"No shit?" Slade spotted the address and parked alongside the curb.

We watched the house for a minute. Inside, a light illuminated the big front window. The curtains were drawn and, through them, we saw two shadows moving together. Like every other house on the street, the garage was closed. I opened my door slightly and heard the faint expression of a saxophone. "We got a jazz geek, Skinny."

Slade cocked his ear and listened. The lonesome notes spilled out across the manicured landscape. Sprinklers came on nearby—a brushing sound in the darkness.

"No doubt Decassin has expensive tastes," Slade said. "You don't get to be a DA's right-hand man if you can't name your varietals."

"Whatever the fuck that means."

"It's wine, Frank."

"Never heard of it."

"You've never heard of wine?"

"Whatever kind you just said. Decassin can keep all that shit to himself for all I care."

Slade shook his head, checked the rearview mirror.

"What's this now?"

I checked the mirror on my side and saw a sleek-looking sports car pulling in behind us. The headlights were off, but I recognized the body style. "Newer Porsche, isn't it?"

"That's right."

I watched in the mirror as the Porsche stopped some twenty feet behind us and the driver's side door opened. A tall white man in a well-cut dark suit climbed out of the car. He looked both ways down the street, closed his door, and approached the back of our shitty Ford.

"Heads up, Skinny. Looks like security, a private detail."

We both stepped out of the Ford at the same time. I kept one hand near my gun. You never know. It can even happen in the manicured, oh-so-perfect country club set. It happens everywhere. And I didn't want to die in a suburb. Frank Pinson, after all the shit he'd been through, deserved to die in the city. Give me that, at least, I thought.

The security man stopped, measured us with a cool, VFA gaze. He sneered and sniffed through one nostril. "You two cops trying to pull something funny?"

Slade lifted a hand in reassurance. "We picked up Turner the other day on something. Just want to have a chat with daddy."

Our playmate guffawed. "Fucking kid. Can't stay out of trouble no matter how much he gets paid. This shit is getting ridiculous." He pressed a finger to his right ear and spoke to somebody in a room somewhere. "The cops are here about the kid. It's no big deal."

Me and Slade looked at each other, swung our heads back at the security guard.

I leaned against the Ford. It swayed with my weight. "You in the service?"

A curt nod. "Two tours in Afghanistan."

"No kidding?"

"I got the shrapnel to prove it." He patted his abdomen. "And now I play rent-a-cop for a big shot. Lot of good my sharpshooting did, huh?"

Slade said, "We thank you for your service."

He said, "Fuck my service. You two can go on up. Just knock on the door."

Slade came around the back of the Ford and we started up the concrete walkway to the front of the house. I looked over my shoulder at the security man as he sat down on the Porsche's front fender. I turned to him with my hands on my hips. "Is there a reason you drive a Porsche around?"

The guy laughed, though it was a sad, short-lived sound. "Decassin thinks it makes us feel special. He wants us to feel like we're guarding the president or some sorry shit. Reminds me of some of these warlord jackasses I ran across in the Middle East." He stood and looked at the car, shook his head. "All this thing does is make me have to shift every three fucking seconds. Plus, they send me for groceries sometimes. It can be a real bitch. I'd rather drive a Prius for fuck's sake. On the job, that is."

"You ever think about City PD?"

"Applied my ass off. Never got past the lie detector portion. You do a lot of bad shit when you're overseas and in...Well, maybe you know, huh?"

"That's too bad," I said moving away from him and shaking my head. "You have a good night now. Enjoy the ride while you're at it."

He flipped a hand like a card dealer telling us we lost a bet. "That, I will do," he said. "And I'll get all the cats from trees and change grandma's underpants, too."

I followed Slade up the walkway. The saxophone got louder, mixed with a piano and steady drums, a maraca somewhere behind all that. Slade pressed the doorbell. Both of us listened for the high-pitched chime.

We were there to see Decassin, but I couldn't keep my eyes off the woman. My balls dropped when she answered the door. Her head reached to about my throat and she wore her brown hair short. It was crinkled up like the ladies used to do in the eighties. Her nose was sharp, but small and cute. High cheekbones ran into leaf-shaped brown eyes. She wore a slip dress—a nice green—that flattened against her hips, slim belly, and thighs. The dress ended above a pair of short white heels. Okay, so she reached to right below my throat. It wasn't too far to bend for a kiss. She didn't say anything, but instead turned and swayed her hips as she led us into the large sitting room. I felt ashamed of myself for enjoying the slow burn in my gut. After all, I still wore my silver wedding band.

Behind me, under his breath, Slade said, "Good God in heaven."

We sat on a low leather couch without armrests. The room was furnished with modern stuff, all of it a shade above uncomfortable. The woman sat in a spacey-looking chair with orange accents and a back that, to me, looked like vinyl or plastic. Decassin sat in a matching chair to her right. He pinched a cigar in one hand and cupped a bottle of European beer in the other—Peroni. He wore trim, dark-colored slacks and a loose-fitting button up. It was unbuttoned to the center of his chest, where black tendrils of hair jutted out like cat's whiskers. His skin was dark brown and he wore his black hair parted to one side.

The jazz was still rolling out across the room. It didn't end until the woman lifted her manicured hands and clapped twice.

The music stopped.

I watched the woman and didn't remember words.

Decassin cleared his throat and nodded at us. "I hear my son has been giving you trouble, detectives." He sipped some Peroni and rolled it inside his mouth, swallowed. A lone trail of sweat ran down the center of his forehead, dripped from the tip of his nose. He wiped it away with the back of his wrist.

I looked at the woman again and held my breath.

Slade said, "That's right, Mr. Decassin. And miss..."

"Portray," the woman said. "Finney Portray."

"Miss Portray," Slade said. "It's a pleasure to meet you." He studied her for too long before shifting his focus back to Decassin. "We came across Turner after he found a man who had been—"

"Murdered," Decassin said. "I know."

"How's that?" At least I found two of my words. I tore my eyes from the clingy green dress and stared at Decassin. It was hot in the house and I began sweating under my arms and beneath my collar. My face still hurt, but the aspirin was working.

"You look as if you've been in a boxing match, Detective. Are you okay?"

I nodded. "It happens. Even to big strong guys like me."

Finney said, "I bet it does." Her voice ran out like hot water.

My balls ached and I knew Slade's did too. Ah, lust—the creature beneath the sea.

Decassin puffed on the cigar and blew smoke over his shoulder. "My son, stepson actually, winds up in the wrong place at the wrong time more frequently than I'd like. He came home two nights ago and told me about the man's...body. He was shaken up, and he seemed genuine that it was nothing involving him. I'm hoping that's still the case."

"But it does involve him," I said, "and it involves you as well, Mr. Decassin."

"How so?"

Slade leaned back on the couch, tried to find a place to rest an arm. He decided to drape his right arm behind me, across the back of the couch. "Dead man happens to be an employee of yours, Mr. Decassin. Gentleman named Enrico Frederico Pablo Castaneda."

I noticed Finney look into her lap as Slade said the name.

Decassin arched his plucked eyebrows. "I'm sorry for the man and his family, but I've never even heard the name. He doesn't work for me, detectives."

"Oh, sure he does," I said leaning forward and placing my elbows on my knees. I swore I smelled lilies and chamomile tea. Finney, maybe. "We know Castaneda didn't fill out an I-9 or nothing, but he sure as shit worked for you."

"I've never heard of him. What was the man's profession? Perhaps I'm mistaken, but—"

"Logistics, I guess you'd call it."

Slade said, "And strategic communication."

For the rough stuff, I thought. "Logistics and strategic communication then."

"My executive assistant handles all my logistical and administrative issues." Decassin shifted slightly in his chair. He puffed on the cigar again and cooled his mouth down with the beer. Beside him, Finney looked at her hands, tried to memorize them.

"Your assistant handles it all, huh?"

"That's right, Detective..."

"I'm Pinson. This is my partner, Ryerson."

"It's a pleasure to meet you both. I'm not sure why you think this man worked for me, but I'm positive you're mistaken. I've never heard the name."

"If you say so," Slade said. "What about the name Applewhite? You ever heard that one?" Finney looked me dead in the eyes. I smiled at her. She started to take slower breaths. Her chest rose and fell with practiced precision.

Decassin glared at Slade. He pinched his cigar and ashes dropped onto the shiny tile floor. "What makes you ask that, Detective Ryerson?"

"Well, not sure if you've heard, but your former business partner, Mark Jacoby, was found dead yesterday. Shallow grave. In the desert. Oh, and the wife and kid, too."

Decassin grunted. "In fact, I did hear about Mark. We weren't partners, however. Both of us had seats on a development board. That's all. I was sorry to hear about him and his family."

"And you didn't think," I said, "that we were coming to chat about him?"

"I had no reason to, Detective. My security detail informed me this concerned Turner."

I tried my best to look surprised. "But you must have had it in the back of your head? I'm curious—how'd you hear about Jacoby?"

"A man named Xander Dames told me. I believe he's a federal agent handling the case."

I rubbed my hands together, thought I was getting somewhere. "Did Dames ask to speak with you about the Jacoby case?"

Decassin placed his cigar in a glass tray on the low glass-topped table between us. He set the beer there too and it made a delicate glass on glass sound. "Why would he need to speak with me in depth, Detective?"

Slade said, "Man's got to cover his bases, am I right?"

"I don't believe," Decassin said, "that I'm any sort of base to cover."

"Tell us about your affiliation with Applewhite." When I said it, Finney stood and stomped into the kitchen. "She don't like that name, huh?"

Decassin's face colored red. He reached into a pants pocket and pulled out a gold necklace, started to fiddle with it in his right hand.

I took this as a nervous tic, what you call a parasympathetic response. A good detective looks for these mannerisms, notices them. A second later, I saw the glinting charm on the end of the necklace as it dangled from Decassin's palm—that damned Santa Muerte. Here she was again. "You pray to the lady?"

Decassin squinted, tilted his head. "It's just a habit, something to help me think. This is a necklace given to me by a friend."

"What friend?"

"I'm beginning to feel like—"

Slade cut him off. "A lying sack of shit?"

Decassin shoved the necklace back into his pocket. "A simple internet search will show I do some political work for Ronald Applewhite. I'm a citizen and I've done nothing illegal."

"So you say," I said.

"I raise money for Applewhite—that's all, Detective."

Slade stood and walked over to a painting on the wall. One of those line and shape drawings they call modern art. I never did become a fan. There were a few other similar paintings hung around the place. I found myself thinking I'd stepped back into the '80s. Decassin had that look about him, the suave gangster dealing in crack cocaine and weapons. Slade put a finger to his chin and said, "What do you suppose this is?"

Finney Portray breezed back into the living room and stood behind Decassin. In her hand, a thin glass of champagne caught the light. She said, "It's not anything. It's just a feeling. Ask yourself what it wants to be."

Slade nodded. "I think it wants to be something it's not."

"Maybe you're right," she said.

"I'd prefer you to practice arts criticism on your own time, Detective. My wife and I—"

"You two are married?" I couldn't believe that I could believe it. But I could.

"Happily," Decassin said. "Are you married, Detective?"

I showed my wedding band, used my other hand to yank the ring off my finger. I held it to the light, examined it. I said, "I used to be, but my wife's dead now. She was distraught." I slipped the ring into my coat pocket and watched Finney's eyes.

She studied me, but gave no sign of her thoughts. She drank from her champagne glass.

"I'm sorry to hear that." Decassin stood and turned to Slade. "If you don't mind, Detective, I'd rather not talk tonight. It's nothing personal, but it seems you've come here under false pretenses. I don't quite appreciate that on a weekend, not with the hours I put in."

Slade turned to watch Decassin.

I stood and smoothed down my wrinkled slacks.

Slade sighed and said, "I think I know what this is: I think it's a big shot drug man trying to make his political chops. I think you want a bigger piece than you've got, Decassin. We don't know why you had Castaneda killed, but we know you're tied into drugs, and that you got ties to possibly the next county DA. We got a lot of dead people with your name in their contact lists. The Jacobys, the Castaneda brothers. In reality, the two of us—Frank and me, I mean—we aren't the smartest men. But we're no dummies either. We're going to burn your ass. I fucking promise you that. When you go to sleep tonight, I know you're going to dream about my handcuffs." Slade slipped a hand behind his back and pulled out the silver bracelets he kept there. They dangled from his hand like good luck charms.

Decassin's face got redder. The color spread to his neck. It showed despite his dark skin. "You two need to get the fuck out of here. And you can go through my lawyer next time. I don't want to see your faces ever again."

We moved to the door and, when we got to it, I turned around and said, "You better get used to me and Slade here, Mr. Decassin. We might be ugly bastards, but we're going to be your only friends come Monday."

"I don't need any pinché friends," he said.

"Oh, come on now," I said, "Even big shots like you need friends, amigo."

As we walked out the door I saw Finney Portray smile. She covered it by taking another sip of champagne.

Chapter 26

The next day, Saturday morning, I woke up with full sun shining bright in my eyes. I reached up from bed and touched the hot window pane with my fingers. True, it wasn't the best weekend for me to sleep in, but Slade said I needed it. My body agreed with him. Hell, I didn't even drink myself to sleep after we met Decassin.

The room was hot.

I whipped the sheets off and saw I was still in my slacks and sport shirt. My tie lay unraveled on the carpet.

It looked to me like a noose.

I stood and slipped the tie around my neck, made a loose knot. On the nightstand, my cell had a text message alert. It was Slade: Coffee at Rodan's. Noon-ish. The time on my cell said it was 11:42 a.m. For once, I wouldn't be late. I brushed my teeth, pissed down the black hole in my bathroom, and walked out into the bright light of Saturday morning.

Rodan's is a little diner off El Cajon Boulevard. It's been there since the forties and, matter of fact, there's an image of JFK pasted onto the side of the building. He's in the back seat of a black convertible Lincoln, cruising down the main boulevard. There's a crowd out to see him, moms and dads and tiny kids waving and smiling at the pretty boy president. A dedication beside the image says that JFK was shot dead in Dallas not six months after visiting our city. Every time I walk by that smiling pretty boy, I think:

What a hell of a shitty way to go.

Slade was hunched into a booth along the street, where the windows looked out on the busy sidewalk and, past that, a wide intersection with decent foot and car traffic—most of it for the transit station a half block north. I slid in across from Slade and waved at the waitress for a cup of coffee. I noticed Slade had something between his arms and, when he looked up at me, I saw it was a newspaper folded to show one half, lengthwise. I noticed his eyes were red-rimmed and knew Slade didn't get much sleep. If any sleep at all.

He sucked air through his teeth and crossed his arms. "You and me are fucked, Frank."

I reached across the table and slid the newspaper to where I could read the headline: "Drug Slayings Confound Homicide Unit." It didn't lead the front page, but it had a prominent spot alongside the main story about the upcoming elections, including a bit about the county DA slot. "How in the fuck did this happen? Was this you, Slade? Your little piece of—"

"You know goddamn well it wasn't me, Frank."

The waitress slammed a coffee mug down in front of me. Black liquid splashed onto the table. She jogged off without cleaning it. I picked up the mug, flipped the newspaper into the puddle of spilled coffee. Brown wetness soaked through the newsprint.

"You're not going to read it?"

"Nope," I said. "Today's the first day in a week I haven't thrown up in the morning. I want to keep it that way."

Slade looked at this watch. "It's half past noon. You can throw up any time."

"How about you just tell me if they have everything." I sipped my coffee and watched people pass outside on the street. It was the regular Mid-City weekend crowd.

Skateboards and beach cruisers and a bum or three shuffling like zombies. A police cruiser sped past, lit up an old Toyota with expired registration.

"It wasn't my lady," Slade said. "But whoever it was, they have almost everything. They left Applewhite out of it, of course. Decassin, too. But they give the Castanedas and say that, in essence, you and me are shit birds who couldn't solve a third-grade crossword puzzle."

"It's just a hit job on us two?"

Slade sipped coffee, coughed hard into his fist. He scratched his unshaven face. "That and a whole section about the drug war, how the violence is spreading and— you know what it is—here we are letting it spread like so much cancer. Point is, Jackson's going to shit himself."

"Might take us off the Castanedas then," I said. "You get a call from the reporter? Nobody called me. I mean, shit, usually they do that much for us. Let us get our say in on the thing."

"My phone died last night after I dropped you off. Woke up this morning to a message about the late deadline and how they were going to run with what they had. Unless I called them back."

"Yeah—that is a fucking hit job."

Slade shook his head.

"You ask girly-girl about it?"

"She thinks they want to put pressure on the chief for some reason. Maybe about some other thing going on. Gave me the old reporter's bail out—can't talk about sources."

I thought about that for a moment. My first headache of the day started to prod at my forehead. I felt the plump part of my face with my index finger, fished out some aspirin from my coat. I slung them into my mouth and chewed, swallowed, chased everything with coffee. "Okay, so they want the brass to talk to them about something, probably some bullshit budgetary concern. Nobody answers their calls, so they—"

"Punch us in the dick," Slade said. "Frank, I swear to God, if I spend another couple years with you, I'm going to be punch-drunk and living out of a Walmart tent down on skid row."

"It's not so bad," I said. "They got tents can withstand hurricane force winds. We'll get you one."

"Bull-fucking-shit."

We sat there for a few minutes wondering how to avoid Jackson. It went without saying that we'd skip the office. Slade had a beaten look to him—he looked like I felt. The aspirin kicked in a little and I felt better. We ordered more coffee and I had some toast with butter. A big part of me wanted to go down to the newspaper and shoot the place up. That might seem extreme, but when you're doing something for the good of others and you get whacked, your sense of proper and improper misfires. After a few more minutes, I said, "What about the man's boots?"

"Who's that?"

"Freddie Castaneda," I said. "Where you think he got those cowboy boots?" The boots bothered me. Had been on my mind—though a low priority—since I first saw them. I knew by the look they were expensive. And the previous night, before I fell asleep, I remembered that Chato wore boots, too. When he came to identify his brother. Different material, sure. Alligator skin, I'd thought.

But expensive and...distinct.

Slade rubbed his forehead. "You're saying we get the brand name and work backwards to some stores in the area? That's some painstaking shit, Frank."

"I don't know, Skinny. What else is there?"

He slid the newspaper back to his side of the table, unfolded it and started reading the opinion pieces. The black coffee stain covered most of the words, but I figured Slade would rather read wet coffee trails than a few thousand words of righteous bullshit.

I remembered I'd done a similar thing on another murder case. It involved a sixteen-year-old girl who went missing. We found a bracelet in her boyfriend's car—tucked between the center console and the passenger seat. He was eighteen and he had a solid alibi. His boss put him out working a construction site on the evening the girl went missing. I followed up on the bracelet because I didn't have shit else. Didn't even have the girl's body yet. Next thing I know, I'm looking at surveillance footage in a little jewelry shop downtown, watching the girl and her boyfriend purchase a gold bracelet. Go figure, it was dated the same night she disappeared. Lot of people don't think this, but a decent lawyer can make something like that seem coincidental, meaningless. It might not matter in a murder trial. Or, maybe it would—there's no guarantee. But a dumbfuck eighteen-year-old doesn't know that. And when you show it to him while he's got his hands cuffed behind his back and a chain wrapped around his ankles, you can bet he's going to do whatever he can to save his ass. All said and done, I doubted his ass was getting saved much up in Pelican Bay.

Maybe, I thought, the boots are like the bracelet.

Probably not. But maybe.

I pulled out my cell and dialed the coroner's office. I had to wait on hold for a few minutes, but I got a newer lab assistant on the line. Not yet weighted down with the cynical humor of a career built on death.

"I'm looking for someone to take a peek at some evidence for me," I said.

"Is it about the drug slayings?"

"Jesus, whoever said these were drug slayings?"

She grunted and said, "It doesn't take Encyclopedia Brown to figure it out."

I asked her to examine the boots worn by both Chato and Freddy Castaneda. She didn't even need to look—the answer burned across her lips. "It's a rare kind of boot. They call them 'El General.' Not crazy expensive, mind you, but pretty hard to find. Here in the US, at least. They could have picked them up in Mexico, though."

"You get all that from Google?"

She said, "Got it before you."

"Thanks for the info." I hung up and tapped Slade's newspaper. "El General boots," I said. "Rare as hog shit in a gold mine. All we have to do is find a local dealer."

Slade folded the newspaper, looked up at me—the

man was as tired as I'd ever seen him. "You can drive, Frank. I'm sick of pretending I have control of shit."

"About time you let loose, Skinny. Maybe now we can have some fun."

Chapter 27

The third boot shop we walked into was a place called Zona Vaquero de Mito. We spotted the tiny storefront and parked illegally in a red zone along the street. The sign above the shop's big dusty window was hand-painted in red and blue. Not very professional. The neighborhood was just south of where Chato was murdered and I figured the location for a place the Castaneda brothers knew. There was a taco shop on one corner, a couple other places selling Quinceañera dresses and piñatas. The boot shop was on the corner, next to Zona Fruta, a local grocery. Slade protested about my parking choice, but I waved him off. Meter maids only drive around the nicer neighborhoods. Maybe Slade was worried about the fire hydrant access.

I opened the door for him and followed into the shop. It smelled of boot black and worn leather. A radio played at low volume behind the front counter—Mariachi—and the boot selection was displayed along the back wall. The array of choices spread from floor to ceiling, one boot displayed from each set. I imagined a back room piled high with solitary boots, all of them longing for their missing twin.

The front counter had a glass case with belts and buckles displayed inside. The cash register was outdated and analog. There were no customers or employees.

I said, "Hola. Anybody here?"

Slade wandered to the boot wall, stared up at it like a man deep inside a canyon. "Maybe I should buy some boots, Frank. What do you think they'd look like with slacks?"

"This ain't the right city for that, Skinny. All the girls will laugh at you."

He shrugged, lifted a suede turquoise-colored model off its shelf. I watched as he smelled the boot's interior, inspected the sole.

A man in his late fifties limped out from the back room. He wore a white cowboy hat and a pair of black leather boots. These below frayed Levi's and a light-colored guayabera. He was fat in the way of older men, not from food or drink, but rather from age and inactivity. He nodded at me, looked at Slade and squinted. "You want some boots, huh? I've been selling here for thirty years. Best boots you can find in the city." He limped behind the cash register and stared at me. "You want some boots for yourself, gordo?"

I didn't take offense. "Matter of fact, I'm looking for a pair of El General boots. Kind of rare."

The man looked down at his case of belts and buckles. He rubbed his thin mustache with one hand. When he looked back at me, I knew he was going to lie. "We don't carry them here in my shop. Too hard to get from Mexico."

Slade came around the front of the counter, leaned on the glass case. He put his face in the boot seller's sweaty-cheeked gaze. "But you know what they are, how to get them if we want them, right? We're not talking regular shipping—all that NAFTA jazz. We're talking how you get them over here for the narcos, amigo."

I smiled—it took a lot for Slade to be so direct and leading. He was pissed, and I found myself thanking the nosy reporters who singed our asses in the morning paper.

The boot seller said, "I don't sell to the narcos."

I spun around and examined the shop. There was an exit sign above the door and few racks of leather jackets up front. The shop windows displayed a couple rows of boots. The other corners of the room looked clean. If there were security cameras, they'd be near the safe, in the back office. I sighed and moved toward the counter. The boot seller watched me with his sweaty face. I reached beneath my coat and removed my 9 mm. I laid the gun on the glass case. It made a funny hollow sound and the boot seller flinched. "Slade, you go ahead and show him the pictures. He can say what he wants about narcos, but we're going to learn what we need to know. Isn't that right, mister…"

"Domingo," he said.

"Mr. Sunday," I said. "Sweet name." My gun felt good in my hand. I liked the warm heavy feel of it against the cold glass.

Slade slipped a printed page out onto the glass. It showed the Castaneda brothers. One image—the one of Chato—was a police mugshot. Enrico's was blown up from his Arizona driver's license. His was more grainy and pixelated.

Domingo didn't swing his chin down to see the page. He looked at it from above his pudgy wet cheeks, with sharp-pointing black eyes. He didn't say anything until I lifted my gun and rested it in my off hand.

"You're a cop. You can't shoot me."

Of course, he was right. Instead, I lifted the gun and smacked him in the ear. It wasn't a particularly violent blow, but I used the butt of the handgun and Domingo toppled backwards, caught himself on the counter. His cowboy hat landed upside down. He bumped into the small radio playing Mariachi music. It fell and shattered on the floor. The music stopped. "It's true I can't shoot you, Mr. Sunday. But I can give you a pretty nasty headache. Is that what you want?" Beside me, Slade was still. I was conscious of his labored breathing, but he knew what needed to happen now. We needed more information and that meant doing some things the law didn't agree with me about.

Domingo straightened. He smoothed down his guay-abera and touched his forehead with two fingers. He stood, left the cowboy hat on the floor. "I sometimes order boots for the gangsters, but it's because they pay me like everybody else. They pay more, sabes?"

"I bet they do," Slade said. "They always order El General boots?"

Domingo nodded. "The same maker, all the time."

I slipped my nine back into my holster. "Who brings the boots to the shop?"

"A woman from Tijuana. I don't know her name. I call a number—a supplier—and she brings them in a truck. It's official, okay? They come wrapped in plastic from the factory, in a box like the boots I get wholesale."

"I bet they do," Slade said again.

I pointed at the images. "These two do the ordering?"

Domingo placed a finger on Enrico's face. "That one

does it. I never saw the other one."

Slade straightened and removed his notepad, started to jot things on the lined paper. "How many boots does this prized customer of yours order, say, weekly?"

Domingo gulped air, looked past us toward the shop windows and the busy street beyond.

I heard sirens somewhere close. "You already decided," I said. "Don't go all mentira on us now."

"Once a week," he said.

Slade made a sound against the roof of his mouth.

"That's a lot of boots," I said.

"This is what I do," Domingo said. He lifted his hands as if surprised. "I'm selling boots to whoever wants a pair of boots."

"How convenient," Slade said as he jotted in his little notebook.

I turned around to look at the street. Two delivery trucks flashed past us. It surprised me to see them on a Saturday. "When's the next delivery for these fancy boots?"

"Today," Domingo said. "Lots of goods coming from Mexico delivered on Saturday. It's a faster time crossing the border."

I nodded and said, "Slade, me and you are going to hang out for a while. I think I want to get me a nice pair of boots."

Slade cleared his throat. "That's a great idea, Frank. Turns out I need a pair, too."

We parked a half block from Mito's and hunkered down to watch. The middle afternoon sun poured into the car and made us both sweat. I removed my tie and

Slade—to my surprise—did the same. We sat there and complained.

"You and me can't get an easy domestic murder, can we?" Slade used a toothpick to clean his teeth. He spat every now and then out the open passenger window. "I mean, shit, all I want is a quick murder rap for a distraught cuckold, okay? I want an open and shut motherfucker, none of this weird cartel shit. You and me hit a bad streak, Frank. All these fucking who-done-its…"

I sighed and rubbed my hand along the hot steering wheel. "You got your big swells and you got your big lulls. Right now, we're looking at a big ass wave and it's about to crash on our heads. We need to solve this motherfucker and—"

"Plural, Frank. Motherfuck-ers."

"Yeah, but it's all tied together. And we know it's Decassin."

"But is it Applewhite?" Slade inhaled, breathed out with exasperation.

"It's always Applewhite," I said. "You look up and down the line, all these murders we've worked, back through the case files…It's fucking Applewhite. Not him personally, fine, but it's people like him. They're out to get something, to take something. And to get there, they have to run through all these people, Slade. Regular fucking people."

"I don't believe that, Frank. You can't just put every act of violence and murder on politicians. That's the blanket theory to the utmost. It's crazy."

I chuckled. "You don't get it, Skinny. You grew up all nice and got yourself a fancy law degree. Shit, you could go and join up with the biggest gang there is—the fucking lawyers."

"Fuck you, fat man."

A few cars crossed through the intersection. There was lots of foot traffic into the grocery beside the boot shop. I counted fifteen mothers with toddlers on their hips, a few construction workers off early, and your regular crowd of grandmothers in Mexican house dresses. No delivery truck yet. I shoved a finger into my mouth and rubbed my gums. Somehow, my face hurt to the teeth. I knew I'd see Johnny around, and I planned to make him pay for my pain.

I said, "It's nothing against you, Skinny. It's just that the whole world is run from the top down."

"You saying a scumbag shoots a kid and it's the president's problem?"

"Fuck the president," I said. "And the whores he rode in on."

"You know what I mean." Slade watched the store too, but he had a dead look in his eyes. I'd seen that look before: It was the Frank Pinson is a dumbass look.

"I'm saying," I said, "that a lot of the shit we see—if not all—has to do with somebody somewhere getting rich. And everybody else getting left behind."

"Spoken by the guy who sent his daughter to a liberal arts school and his son to a pretty decent law school. You're part of the fucking problem, waving a goddamn nine around like it's a lollipop. Isn't it you in that video pounding some fool into unconsciousness?"

"I've done good work in my career." My neck and eyeballs started throbbing with anger. I loved Slade to death, but he knew how to piss me off, and he was smarter than me. "Put more wretched souls behind bars than most other cops."

"And by your theory," Slade said, "you haven't done a fucking thing."

I thought about Decassin sitting in that chair, the lit cigar smoking in his hand. I thought about him kissing Finney Portray, about her letting him do it. I thought about my wife soaring downward toward blackened water as hard as cement. "I get Applewhite, and Decassin, then I've done something. And maybe you're right. All those scumbags before this were nothing. They were a way to get to here, to right now."

"And the way you tell it, not a damn thing will be solved. Besides, Decassin killed a couple narcos with blood on their hands, Frank. It's not like we're after a cop killer."

"No, we're not," I said as a white delivery truck pulled alongside the boot shop. Black spray paint—gang tagging—decorated the cargo hold, and the driver's side door was gray, a replacement from a different vehicle. A young woman in Levi's, a purple halter top and sandals climbed out, went around back. She lifted the cargo door and stood there with her hands on her hips. Mr. Sunday limped out of the store, stood beside her on the sidewalk. "We're after some drugs, Slade," I said, "and the bullshit artists who prance around spending money they make off those same drugs." I slipped my finger beneath the latch, swung my door open into the street.

As I moved down the sidewalk, one hand pressed to my holstered gun, I caught myself praying that Slade decided to follow me. Funny thing, I wasn't praying to God—I prayed to the sweet lady of death herself. I prayed to Santa Muerte.

* * *

The young woman spotted me as I jogged, hand on my gun, down the sidewalk. A short expression of surprise crossed her face—raised eyebrows and terse lips—before she hopped onto the truck's bumper, slammed the cargo door back down into place, and sprinted to the cab. She flung the gray door open and vaulted into the driver's seat.

The engine started as I shouted: "Police! Don't move! Don't move!"

The truck pitched and rumbled. The woman popped the clutch, restarted the engine and accelerated down the street. I touched the cargo door just as she found the throttle. A puff of black smoke shot from the muffler and surrounded me like a misshapen shadow.

I eyeballed Domingo and he shrugged. Women were running out into the street from the fruit market, everybody looking at me with hatred—that's what the police get in neighborhoods like this. Maybe it's the proper reaction. Who am I to judge? I turned and saw Slade sprinting back to the car. I holstered my gun while he hopped into the driver's seat, punched the gas and slid to a stop beside me. We were squealing down the street before I had my door closed. "She fucking saw me before I—"

"We could have drove up on her," Slade said. "Fuck, Frank." He reached across his body and pulled down his seat belt, buckled it. "She better not get away. Call this in, man."

"Take a right here. Go, Skinny."

The Ford rattled and creaked. We flew past more shops and auto repair places, came out onto an industrial street. A long metallic window reflected our path as we burned down the street. I was conscious of the reflection, though I never turned to see it.

A small sedan changed lanes and I spotted the truck one block ahead. It ran a yellow light and turned left, toward the nearest highway entrance—headed south. "Go left at the light and make the next right. We need to cut her off at the freeway entrance."

Slade ignited the siren in our windshield and swung us left at the light. Loose change rattled in the center console and my teeth clicked as we crossed a rough patch of road. Slade hit a deep pothole and the front end crunched.

"Fuck," he said and punched harder on the gas.

He made the next right and I saw the truck just ahead, making a right turn on the next block.

"Call in air support, Frank. We need backup on this. Get some patrol officers here, man."

"Fuck that." I rolled down my window. Hot air slapped me in the face and my eyes dried as Slade accelerated. I licked my lips. "Pull alongside her."

"Frank, I can't just—"

"Hit the fucking gas, Skinny!"

The engine roared again, surged in protest as the transmission dropped a gear, shot us forward alongside the moving truck. I saw the woman through the window. Her eyebrows were furrowed and her mouth was pushed up against her nose. Her bare shoulders hunched forward into the steering wheel. She turned to look at me—I pulled my 9 mm and pointed it at her.

"Jesus-fuck, Frank. What the—"

"Pull over, amiga! Pull the fuck over!"

I saw her consider my polite request. The truck's engine let off for a moment, gave a slight tinge of deceleration. Fear crossed the woman's face and—I imagined—a thousand thoughts ran through her brain. I wondered if, like Rambo, she was dead already. Was El Jefe on her ass and about to smoke her for talking to the cops? I didn't doubt it, not after seeing the dead Castaneda brothers.

The woman's mouth unclenched and the truck slowed. She downshifted and the brakes squealed. She pulled to the curb on a one-way street, just shy of the freeway entrance. Traffic spun past on the elevated highway.

The truck's engine gasped as the woman again popped the clutch. I was out of the Ford before Slade stopped, my nine still raised, its oh-so-certain gaze pointed through the window at the woman.

I opened the door for her—that's the kind of man I am.

Part Three

Chapter 28

Jackson sneered as Slade pulled another stack of cash and another brick of coke from another pair of El General boots. We were at the station, in a hot ass conference room, unpacking the boxes from the moving truck. The stack of money was about a foot high and two feet long—going on close to two million in legal fucking tender.

The coke I didn't keep track of, but it was a lot.

Jackson said, "Jesus fucking Christ almighty in heaven. You imagine how much of this shit gets through? You two nailed this on a hunch, a fucking guess?"

He breathed hard through his mouth and I smelled cigarette smoke.

Slade kept searching boots and I nodded at Jackson. "Luck, Captain. Pure luck."

"What's the girl saying?"

I said, "She's going to lawyer up. You know how it is. She isn't saying shit."

"And the boot salesman, the old fuck?"

"Same deal," I said. "Cartel's got the best lawyers money can buy." I motioned at the roomful of boxes. "Best boots, too."

Jackson hefted a stack of plastic-wrapped cash, felt the weight of it. "I want to know what the money's for." He rubbed the back of his head, tossed the money back on the stack. "What you see most times, it's the drugs coming this way and—"

"The money going that way," Slade said.

I sat down in a rolling office chair, put my feet on the table. "It's probably a payment, or a donation for a political action committee. Great way to hide the money, right Slade?"

Slade rolled his eyes. "Damn you, Frank."

"What now? What's all this shit about a political action committee?" Jackson looked from me to Slade. His cheeks got red. "Ryerson, what the fuck? A PAC for who?"

I stood again and crossed my arms. "We have it that the Castaneda brothers were ordered murdered by Regis Decassin, a big-time fancy developer. Turns out Decassin runs a PAC for Ronald J. Applewhite, attorney at law."

Jackson pinched the bridge of his nose, rubbed his forehead. "They were 'ordered murdered by,' Frank? The fuck does that mean? You're dabbling in all this political—"

"We're saying Decassin did it, but he didn't pull the trigger."

"You think you're working a mob case? You think it's the 1920s, Frank?"

Slade said, "We put it together and it's legit." He slid a pair of boots to the side, pulled out his notebook and slapped it on the table. "You want the whole thing right now?"

"Do I want the whole thing right now? No—I don't

want any of it. I know you two saw the paper, and you're hoping I don't bring it up. We got a city calling these Castaneda her-mon-ohs the drug brothers. You're telling me it's a high society thing? I don't want a goddamn thing to do with it. That's where the fuck I'm at." He breathed as deep as he could, leaned back in the chair with his arms behind his head. "I don't want a fucking thing."

"This is how it goes," I said.

Jackson shook his head. "What about a trigger man?"

Slade sighed. "Need a murder weapon."

"It's probably at the bottom of the sea by now," Jackson said.

"Then we follow the money." I pointed at Slade. "We got him, and the two of us follow the money."

Jackson said, "He'll be dragging you around on a leash."

"I'm a good boy," I said.

"I don't want to read anymore news stories like what I got today. Zip it, motherfuckers. That means you, lover boy." Jackson glared at Slade. "Keep me updated, assholes. And I'm sending the techs in to inventory this stuff. You two can get your grubby hands off that money."

"And drugs," Slade said.

"That too, detectives."

Slade slid his last taco toward me. We were at a taco shop uptown and I was still hungry. I shifted in the booth, nodded at Slade, and pinched the taco with two fingers. It went down the gullet—nothing to it. "Thanks,

Skinny."

No response.

"I'm stress eating."

"You're stressed? Shit. I'm about to pry my own eye-balls out."

"Let's not be dramatic." Out the window, across the street, there was a contemporary-style office building. On the windows were two names: Applewhite and Lamonte. "We see the man go in and we just walk right in," I said.

"Meet him in his office for a little chat."

"A pleasant discussion."

"A polite palaver."

"College boy," I said. Fucking vocabulary.

Slade looked at his hands, spun his cell on the table. He watched it until it stopped, went back to watching the law offices of Applewhite and Lamonte.

My own cell buzzed in my pocket. I looked at the number and said, "Oh, shit."

"Who is it?"

"It's Kimmie."

"Better answer that one, papi."

I pressed the answer button and put the phone to my ear.

"Hey there, sweetheart."

"Daddy?"

"What is it, honey?"

"Are you alone?"

I looked at Slade, lifted my finger to my lips. "Yeah, honey. I'm just having some lunch."

She sniffed and exhaled.

"Are you crying, Kimmie?"

She didn't respond.

"Kimmie? Everything okay, honey?"

"You won't be mad at me, will you?"

I thought for a second—did she run off and get married to that blonde chick? "I've never been mad at you a day in my life." I placed a hand on the table, flattened my palm. I listened to my daughter cry and I waited.

Slade watched me, interested.

"I'm pregnant, Daddy."

I sat in silence, rubbed my hand in a slow circle. My eyes shot to Slade and back down to my hand. I started to speak, but Kimmie interrupted me.

"I knew you'd be—"

"That's exciting, Kimmie."

"What?"

"I'm thrilled to hear it. I can't wait. It better be a boy."

Slade leaned back in the booth, watched me with a smile.

"I thought you'd be mad."

"Why the hell would I be mad?"

"I don't know..."

"One thing I wonder, though," I said. "How'd you—"

"My boyfriend."

My saliva caught in my throat. I choked. "But I thought you were a—"

"Lesbian? Oh, Daddy—that was just a phase."

Applewhite arrived forty minutes later. That was okay. He gave me time for three more tacos. Al pastor, pineapple, and cilantro. Nothing like it. We saw Applewhite come around the building from the parking area and stroll in the glass front doors. The receptionist stood and smiled for him. "You see what car he's driving?"

Slade shook his head. "No, I missed it."

I slid from the booth and loosened my belt a notch. "Nothing like a little taco siesta, huh?"

We crossed the street outside the taco shop and entered the law office. The high-powered air conditioning was pleasant. Slade started in on the receptionist while I studied the building's directory etched onto a marble wall. The partners' offices were on the third floor.

I walked toward Slade as he was leaning into the receptionist's ear, whispering about Padres tickets and a nice seafood dinner. "Don't believe any promise this man makes," I said. "I'm the one you want. I might be big, but I'm happy."

The receptionist, a well-fed twenty-something with pretty blue eyes, laughed and bit her bottom lip. "Detective Ryerson was just saying how he couldn't live without you."

I laughed. "Is that right?"

"He says you're looking for a date." She stared right at me. "Is that right?"

Slade straightened his tie. "I was saying how you wouldn't mind taking Miss Patterson here out for dinner, that is, if she was willing to arrange a brief palaver with Mr. Applewhite. How's that sound, Frank?"

I smiled at the receptionist. "Tell you what, you get us a quick sit down with Applewhite, and me and you are going to dine on the waterfront."

She sighed and pointed at my wedding ring. "I'm thinking you're taken, Detective, but Mr. Applewhite has made it clear that law enforcement officers are always welcome to see him. You two can go on up—third floor right."

I twisted my ring and shrugged. "Never hurts to flatter a woman, does it?"

"No," she said, "it doesn't."

Me and Slade walked to the bank of elevators. Neither of us said anything while we waited. The receptionist hummed a tune to herself.

Soon, a sharp ring sounded and the elevator arrived.

Applewhite was waiting to greet us when the elevator opened. "Detectives, it's a pleasure to have you here in my office."

The three of us shook hands and Applewhite led us through a professionally decorated foyer, past an assistant's well-lit office, and into a corner office overlooking the city skyline. Applewhite motioned for us to sit and we took two leather chairs across from him. He sat cross-legged in a large office chair. Applewhite wore a blue bow tie and a white button-down beneath an off-gray vest. His clothes were obviously tailored and I found myself wondering how much his facials cost him. He had perfectly tanned skin, his hair parted artfully to one side, and fingernails as perfect as a mannequin's. I didn't like the man one fucking bit.

Slade said, "Mr. Applewhite, we're here about—"

Applewhite lifted a smooth hand and said, "Let me first say I really appreciate the work our police force is doing here in this great city. I know you have a difficult job, detectives. A loathsome trying job in its dealings with death. I am in complete awe of the dedication, perseverance, and expertise of our law enforcement officers. Not least our crack detectives. For both of you, your reputation precedes you." He touched a folded newspaper on his desk. "I find it appalling how the press has treated you both in today's paper. And without seeking comment. It's utterly despicable and indefensible. Know this: if elected district attorney, I will stand behind my officers through thick and thin, notwithstanding the press's veiled attempts at character assassination. I hope you know that I have your backs, gentleman. Now, and always."

"That's heartwarming, sir," I said.

Slade grunted.

"Now," Applewhite said, "what can I do for you gentleman?"

"You can tell us about your relationship with Regis Decassin." Slade smiled as he said it.

"Come again?"

"Regis Decassin," I said. "You know, a cartel money launderer here in the city?"

"I'm afraid I've never heard of the man."

Me and Slade nodded.

"If you're implying that I am, in some way, involved with this man, I must insist—"

"There's nothing to imply," I said. "But there sure as shit is plenty to infer."

Slade added, "The man runs a PAC for you, doesn't he?"

Applewhite's face screwed into anger. "I've got nothing to do with any PAC. As you may know, political action committees operate independent of candidates. For me to be involved would be not only unethical, but also a—"

"Violation of campaign finance and election laws,"

Slade said.

I chuckled and pointed at Applewhite. "You mean, you'd be a crook?"

The three of us sat in silence for a long while, though I thought I heard Applewhite's blood boiling.

I ended the silence. "You want to talk about Decassin?"

"I've never heard of the man."

"Let's be clear," Slade said. "Me and Frank here have done some digging, and I think it highly likely that you and Decassin—"

"Must I have a lawyer present?"

"You are a fucking lawyer," I said.

"Detectives," Applewhite said, "it's likely that in the next couple months I'll become—in a way—your boss. I'd warn you against any efforts at undue investigations. Now, if I can help you with an ongoing investigation, I'm happy to—"

"Where'd you grow up?" Slade cleared his throat. "Around here somewhere?"

"I was born in Los Angeles."

"We hear you," I said, "but where'd you grow up—where'd you pop your cherry?"

"What does that have to do with—"

"Please, Mr. Applewhite. Indulge us."

Applewhite uncrossed his legs, rolled his chair closer to the desk. "I spent most of my childhood in Mexico. In Juarez. My father worked in El Paso. It was cheaper living across the border."

We both nodded.

Slade said, "No need for a man to apologize about where he comes from."

Applewhite scowled. "I wasn't apologizing for it."

"Of course not," I said. "Why would you?"

"Do you two jerks have something you want to discuss aside from half-formed ideas about political corruption?"

Slade acted surprised. "Oh, wow. Who the hell ever said anything about political corruption?"

"Not me," I said.

"Me neither," Slade said.

Applewhite pointed a gaze at each of us and shook his head. He sighed and said, "You two get the fuck out of here—I don't want to hear about this again. And I'll be giving captain…"

"Jackson," I supplied, "Captain Jackson."

"I'll be giving Captain Jackson a call about this."

Me and Slade stood. Applewhite didn't move. I bowed like a karate fighter. "It's been a pleasure, Mr. Applewhite. Thanks for your time."

Applewhite said, "The pleasure has been all yours."

About that, he was right.

Chapter 29

Back outside, with the receptionist watching us through the glass doors, Slade sniffed hard and said, "The man's from Juarez. You believe that?"

"We are a nation of immigrants."

"What I'm thinking about is the witness from Chato's murder."

"The gangbanger?" I coughed and taco meat bounced in my stomach.

"Didn't he say something about the vehicle, the sticker on the back window was—"

"That's right," I said. "Fucking Juarez."

We followed the sidewalk around the building, found a covered parking lot accessed via ramp from the street. There was no gate. Me and Slade strolled right in and started to look for a silver Mercedes. It didn't take long. In the back row of spots, all reserved for lawyers according to the placards, was a dusty silver Mercedes with a large sticker on the back window. The sticker spelled Juarez in a lightning bolt font.

Slade stood with his hands on his hips and shook his head.

I wandered over to the car and squinted to see

through the tinted windows.

"We need to get us a warrant, Frank." Slade peered into the windows on the passenger side. I couldn't see much inside but the shape of the front seat and a center console. I tried the front door, jostled the handle.

"Frank, dammit. Don't touch it."

"Just want a quick look," I said.

And then Applewhite's voice echoed across the parking garage. "Look with your eyes and not your hands, Detective."

Slade said, "Fuck me, man."

Applewhite walked up on us and laughed. "If I fuck you, Detective...it'll be in a courtroom. Now you two get the fuck out of here. I just had a civil chat with Captain Jackson—he thinks you might want to reimagine your puny theory about these murders."

"Is that right?" I stomped over to Applewhite and put my face next to his. "You think some wannabe DA has sway over a hard-nosed cop?"

"Could be," Applewhite shrugged. "If not, there are lots of ways to persuade him."

"Oh, really?"

"Really, Detective Pinson. Now, please..." Applewhite pivoted and lifted his hand at the exit. As we walked out onto the sun-bleached street, Slade had his cell to his ear.

We needed to call Jackson.

We'd been summoned.

Jackson pinched the bridge of his nose, like he did the day before when he showed me the video. His desk was covered with the day's newspaper edition and a stack of manila folders. The desk looked like Jackson had dumped everything on its surface at once. Mixed in were random notes on lined paper and two paper coffee cups. He planted his elbows in the mess and said, "You two numbskulls are going to fuck me. If it's the last thing you do, you're going to fuck me."

"Captain," Slade said, "we need a warrant on the Benz. That's all."

"That's all? Fuck you, Ryerson. I need a warrant for your ass."

"That's odd, Captain." I smiled as I said it.

Jackson stood and swept his arms across the desk. The papers and coffee cups fell to the floor in a rustling wave. He slammed his palms down on the desk. "You assholes are fucking with my life, goddammit!"

"How the fuck is that?" I didn't mark Jackson for crooked, but now I wondered.

"Applewhite's gonna be the new DA, assholes."

Slade said, "On some corrupt campaign donations."

Jackson's face reddened and shimmered with sweat. "And it's all legal, fuckwad. You fuckers realize Applewhite didn't squeeze a fucking trigger in these murders. He didn't cut off our dead man's junk. He didn't chop off the man's fingers—he didn't do a fucking thing."

I stood and smoothed down my shirt. "Maybe not, but he knows who the fuck did. And why."

Jackson pointed a fat index finger at me. "You, Frank, are done here. You're fucking—"

"I'm done? How's that?"

"You're fucking suspended, Pinson."

"Captain, what the—"

"Go to hell, Ryerson," Jackson said.

My own face got red. I felt the heat burn up to my

eyes. "You wouldn't dare."

"I got two minutes of police brutality that says I will."

"You know that video's a personal fucking thing."

Jackson shrugged. "What do we call it...Conduct unbecoming? Is that how you want me to write it out in the report? I'm open to your interpretation, Pinson."

My stomach swirled against itself. I thought I might vomit.

"You're a drunk, Pinson. You couldn't solve a ten-piece jigsaw puzzle."

"Twenty-four fucking years," I said.

"Me too, Frank. And you're trying to fuck me."

Slade stood and moved to the door, rested his hand on the latch. He looked back at Jackson and said, "How much?"

"How much what?" Jackson kept his fat eyes on mine while he spoke.

"How much are they paying you to keep Applewhite out of it?"

"Good luck trying to prove that."

"Fuck proof," I said. "There's truth and lies—they're all that matter."

Jackson sank into his chair. He laced his hands behind his head and sighed. He licked his plump lips and kept staring at me. "It's you or me, Frank. That's all I got to say."

I nodded.

Slade opened the door and walked out cursing.

Jackson said, "I got kids, man. A wife. I got shit I want to do and it's only a few more months until I get out of this. It's not personal, Frank. I swear it's not—"

"You'll die a sad death," I said. "I can see it for you.

Sad and lonely."

Jackson unlaced his hands and placed one on his service weapon. "Is that a threat?"

"No. It's just a little bit of truth for you. Consider it a gift." I left my badge on his desk.

Chapter 30

Slade stood in the bathroom doorway and stared at my home improvement wreckage. "You still haven't installed this damn toilet? What the hell, Frank? Where you do you take a shit, partner?"

"Used to be the station," I said from the kitchen where I poured us both some bourbon. I walked into the living room and handed Slade a glass. He followed me and we sat. I took the couch and Slade took the easy chair in the corner. "Now I'm going to have to try the public library."

"Or you can install the toilet."

"You know what brand that is? American Standard. Think about that, Slade. What the fuck is an American Standard?" I sipped bourbon and tried to suppress the anger boiling up through my belly. I wanted to kill Jackson. And not for the suspension, but because he was so clearly corrupt. I couldn't believe it—the surprise was the closest I'd felt to when I got the news about Miranda.

Vague numbness followed by incredible nausea.

And anger.

"Depends on what American you're talking about. And what standards. You know?"

"So, what now?" I finished my glass, got up for more.

Slade lifted his hand to stop me. "We have work to do, Frank."

"You have work to do."

"The fuck I do. This isn't over. And now it's about this." Slade tapped the badge dangling from his neck. "It's about right and wrong, all the shit in between too."

I sat back down, clanged my glass on the coffee table. "If Jackson killed it...Shit. We got shit."

"We tried Applewhite, Decassin. I say we take it back to the streets. Where everybody knows everything, but nobody says anything. We need to find that Rambo kid again. He can get us somewhere. I know he can."

"We already tried to—"

"The legal fucking way," Slade said. "But you, Frank...You're off that motherfucking clock."

I sat there and stared at the open bathroom door, the new toilet gleaming white and porcelain beside it. I've been pissing down a hole, I thought. Like a monkey in the fucking jungle. I shook my head, leaned back into the couch. I took a long breath and closed my eyes. "You saying we do what we need to do, however it needs to get done?"

Slade's voice sounded hollow across the room. "I'm saying you're independent and I'm a trusted advisor. If, of course, that's how we need to do it."

Yeah, right. I opened my eyes and leaned forward, stared daggers at my former partner. His badge shined in the late afternoon sun. "Back to the street. Rambo, then," I said. "Let's go and find his ass."

* * *

Back on the streets of the downtrodden. Slade slid alongside a place called Reggie's Strip Palace. I'd never been, but Slade had a CI who ran numbers in the back, a guy named Cid. According to Slade, Cid had his fingers on all the low-level action in the city. If anybody knew where Rambo was hiding, or whether he was still alive to be found, it was Cid. Or Cid knew who the fuck would know. Me and Slade both checked our weapons and holstered up. I was curious about where all this was going to take us, but I wasn't nervous.

I said, "You think Cid's going to try and do us wrong?"

"I been knowing Cid for a long time. The man works for money."

"But we don't have any to give him."

"Not like he has to know that."

"Right," I said. "A little white lie."

"Or two," Slade said as he exited the car.

We nodded at the bouncer as we walked into the place. I knew he radioed our presence right away. It was easy to see we were cops. Not easy to see? That one of us was no longer acting as a cop. You know, suspension and all. We walked down a dark hallway scented with vomit and pre-ejaculation. I tasted bile on my tongue and Slade coughed until we entered the strip club's interior. There was a large stage with two stripper poles in the center. A low bar with cracked leather seats surrounded the stage. There were two smaller stages—platforms, really—off to each side, both with single gold poles. The bar ran along back, next to a wall of purple curtains that I knew must lead to private rooms. Sparse lighting from a strobe and loud hair rock through the speakers. No girls on the side stages. But there was one girl on the center stage. She had her ass in the air and it jiggled until she stood, arched her back, and swirled like a vixen. Her tits were tan with dark nipples. Her G-string might as well have been dental floss. When I finished memorizing her body, I squinted through the darkness and tried to see the girl's face. "Wait a minute, Slade."

"What's up, Frank?"

I moved forward through the empty cocktail tables and grimy booths. There was a step down toward the stage and I nearly stumbled over it. I caught myself and cleared my throat. Ten or so creepy losers surrounded the stage, almost all wearing bent trucker hats or flat-brimmed baseball caps pulled low over prying eyes.

"What the fuck, Frank? You falling in love?"

I could feel Slade close behind me and I shook my head. "You've got to be shitting me."

"What, man?"

"It's her," I said. I knew the pink hair. And that pouty teenage girl look. Our conversation about her lawyer daddy echoed somewhere in my head.

"Who?"

"Celeste fucking Richards. Turner's girlfriend. That's who."

"You gentlemen need some assistance?"

I turned around to face another bouncer, this one made of hard muscle and prison terms. He had a buzzcut, but I saw his prison facial expression even in the dark.

Slade crossed his arms and said, "We're here to have a chat with Cid. He around?"

"Who the fuck are you?"

My mind raced and my blood thickened. I stepped in front of Slade and looked the bouncer up and down, clenched my fists. "The guys who are going to do your dental work."

Slade placed a hand on my chest, stepped in front of me. "Hey, look, I'm an old pal of Cid's. Just tell him Skinny came in for a chat. It's nothing serious. I promise, he knows me. Forget about my buddy here...He's having a bad day."

The bouncer glared at me over Slade's head. "Threaten me again, and you'll have yourself a bad life, asshole." He looked down at Slade and said, "Give me a minute."

I watched him walk past the bar and vanish behind one of the purple curtains. Slade turned and nodded at the stage. "You're sure that's her?"

I turned around, sank into a booth. I watched Celeste as she shook her ass some more, did a naked pirouette—hair waving all around her face—and dry-humped the stripper pole. "Jesus H fucking Christ, Slade. It's her...yeah, it's her."

Slade took in the girl's body and shrugged. "Sometimes you got to shake your moneymaker."

I watched Celeste and swore she put her eyes on mine. She rubbed her midsection up and down the pole, slow-pranced across the stage, and disappeared as the song ended. A bunch of guys threw dollar bills onto the stage and another girl in tight jeans and a halter top appeared on stage and scooped the bills into a bucket. I closed my eyes and breathed as deep as my lungs allowed.

The bouncer reappeared from behind the purple curtain and waved to us.

Slade said, "Let's go, Frank. Try to forget about the girl."

Cid Miser wore a silver grill in his teeth, talked like he knew one too many rappers, and didn't take his eyes off the calculator in front of him. One of those calculators accountants use—it had a roll of white paper on the top and kept churning out numbers and equations. He didn't look up at us as he greeted Slade. "What up, Skinny? My boy said you want to chat." He kept punching numbers. His bouncer leaned against the wall to my left, beside a large flatscreen television tuned to ESPN. "Busy with business," Cid said, "get to it."

"Looking for somebody," Slade said. "It's important."

"How important?"

"Five bills important."

The number punching stalled for a second, started back up as Cid said, "If it's worth five bills to you, it's worth a G to me."

"Consider it done. If you put us on the right trail."

"This someone got a name? Or a street handle?"

"Goes by Rambo," I said. "Like the movie."

"Who the fuck's your friend here, Skinny?" Cid wagged a finger at me.

Slade said, "This is my partner, Frank."

"That right? I hear he got an attitude."

"That's fair." I moved closer to Cid's desk, sensed the bouncer close beside me. "And I hear you got an underage girl working the stage."

"Hey, Reg," Cid said, "what's goofy dude's name

plays basketball down at the Y?"

"Sunday, open gym?"

"Yeah, man."

The bouncer said, "Call him Rambo, on the streets."

"That right?" Cid stopped punching the calculator and his eyes looked like obsidian in the dark office. "Funny, what's today?"

"Sunday," I said.

"The goddamn sabbath." Cid smiled at me and the silver grill flashed. "Day of rest, man."

Skinny's hand dug into my shoulder.

I straightened. "What about the girl?"

"You want to save her ass, go on and be my guest, five-oh." He went back to punching numbers on the calculator.

I swiveled and threw my right fist into the bouncer's stomach. He doubled-over with a grunt and I brought my knee to his forehead. I swung my left elbow like a sledgehammer and it connected with the back of the bouncer's neck. He crumpled up like tissue, lay gasping on the floor.

Slade said, "Fuck, Frank."

Cid finished whatever numbers he was punching and leaned back in his chair. There was a long silence as the bouncer gasped for air and Cid stared at me. He looked at Skinny, raised his eyebrows, and looked back to me. "You a big boy, huh? You looking for a part-time job? I got a lot of tough motherfuckers come in here and try to grab the girls. I pay—"

"Go fuck yourself."

"Hey, whatever, man. Don't come crawling back to me when that fucking pension ain't enough."

Slade grabbed at me again and said, "Thanks for the

lead, Cid."

Cid went back to punching numbers. "I'll take that G by the end of the week."

"Drive around back, Skinny."

"What now, motherfucker?" Attitude in his voice.

"Drive us around back—I want to see something."

Slade shook his head in disgust, but he slid the Ford into an adjacent alley and boxed around the strip club. We came out on a parking area full of used-new economy cars. The fucking stripper fleet. I saw a couple girls next to a propped open door. They were in sweatpants and hoodies, all smoking and laughing together. Again, I recognized Celeste.

Slade pulled the car alongside the girls.

I reached back and unlatched the back door. It swung open and Celeste rolled her eyes. I motioned for her to come over and she did the walk of shame while the other girls giggled or gave us snotty looks. Celeste scrunched into the back seat and closed the door.

"What's wrong, Detective? Never seen a naked chick before?"

"Not one your age," I said. "Unless she was dead."

Slade made a noise in his throat.

"What's that supposed to mean?" Celeste puffed on her cigarette, unlatched the door, and tossed the cigarette outside. She closed the door again and sighed.

"It means," I said, "that you're on the wrong fucking path."

"You know, you should have been a guidance counselor."

"Shit," Slade said. "Man couldn't counsel a—"

"Shut it, Skinny." I shifted in my seat, tried to face Celeste. I was too big in the seat and only got one eye on her. It was enough to see the pouty lips and puffed-up eye sockets. "I want you to quit this shit, Celeste. I'm serious. You want a job, I'll help you find one."

"I don't want a job. I want my own money."

"But this is—"

"Easy money," she said. "They can look, but they don't touch."

"Until they do," I said.

"Can I go now?"

Skinny shrugged and I turned back to look out the windshield. One of the strippers sauntered in front of our car, chirped the alarm on a Toyota and climbed inside it. She backed out and zoomed down the alley.

I sighed and said, "I'm coming back in a week. You better be gone."

"Whatever, Detective." Celeste opened the door.

Slade looked back at her before she got out. "You seen your boyfriend lately?"

"Turner's gone. He left two nights ago."

"No shit? Where'd lover boy get off to?"

"Where the fuck you think?" Celeste said. "Juarez. You know, Mexico?"

Chapter 31

A volley of hardwood squeaks and shouts filled the basketball gym in the Mid-City Y. I took a seat on the metal bleachers, watched the game with all the guys waiting for their turn to play. The game was full court, five-on-five, and Rambo—like when we chased him down—ran around like he had four lungs. I was surprised at how good the kid played. He was a natural point guard with court vision and a decent mid-range jumper. I raised my eyebrows at Slade who stood near the closest exit. He shrugged and put his hands out as if to say, We all have our talents. At point game, Rambo yo-yo'd the ball up court and found a big man for a low post score. The team celebrated with ass slaps and high-fives. Rambo jogged over to the bleachers for a swig of his sports drink. When he did, I started clapping.

He looked up at me and said, "Shit, man."

"You look like you played college ball, Rambo," I said. "That's impressive."

"I played juco ball, upstate." He wiped sweat off his head with a T-shirt and glared at me.

"Funny. You might get a chance to play upstate again. Different competition though."

"C'mon, man. You know I'm not what you're looking for."

I motioned toward the exit. Rambo noticed Slade and called to a few buddies that he'd be back. He pointed at another guy to fill in for him. Outside, me and Slade stood close to Rambo as he leaned against the Y's stucco wall. We were in the parking lot and Rambo's eyes flitted over the nearby cars.

"What you fuckers want with me, man? You know I'm nothing—not compared to what you want."

"You didn't kill anybody then?" Slade leaned in and sniffed Rambo's neck. "I smell lies."

"Fuck no. I'm the one's going to get killed. Especially if—"

"Why you still in town then?"

Rambo said, "Where am I going to go? Everything I got, it's here. I haven't been back to my place. I'm staying with a lady friend out in east county."

"I thought," I said, "that you were dead. Isn't that what you said?"

Rambo's eyes skirted the parking lot again. "Might be still. Unless these fuckers forget. You two aren't helping me, man. I swear to God."

He tried to walk away from us, but I stepped to one side and Slade closed off the other.

"Unless who forgets?" I said.

Rambo sighed, started to shake his head. He leaned back against the wall, wiped sweat from his right cheek. "The cartel, man—Juarez."

"You work for them?"

"Look, I sell street drugs. Okay? You want, take my ass in." He put his wrists together and held them out for us to take. Slade rolled his eyes and I laughed. "Okay then," Rambo said. "I work for Turner, and that's it. Fucking kid keeps me supplied and I pay him back. It's some low-level shit. I fucking lease my car, man."

A look of confusion crossed Slade's face. "Turner is your connect?"

I scanned the parking lot myself. Bunch of beaters and a few Hondas made to look like they were fast and furious. No silver Mercedes and no black SUVs with mysterious-looking gangsters.

"Yeah, man. Has been for the last year or so."

Slade said, "What about that night, when you dropped Turner and the girl off under the bridge?"

"It's like we said: Turner didn't want to drive because he was high as fuck."

"What about the Jacoby murders? You brought those up," Slade said.

"Because Turner told me to."

I felt my own look of surprise surface on my face. "The fuck you saying?"

Slade chuckled and said, "Why would he do that?"

"The fuck if I know," Rambo said, shrugging. "Only thing I can think is he wanted to impress his girl." He stared at us with big unknowing eyes. "I ain't the fucking detective."

Celeste's naked body passed through my mind. And then I saw the expensive house where I dropped her off on the night—no, early morning—of the first Castaneda murder. "You're saying Turner told you specifically to bring up the Jacoby murder?"

"Name and fuck-all," Rambo said. "Gave me a hundred bucks to do it."

Slade turned around, walked a few steps with his hands on his head. "Fuck me, man."

"And you think he did it to impress the chick?"

"I don't know no other reason. What the fuck she know about murder and all these drugs?"

Slade came back and said, "It is confusing."

"Maybe not so much," I said.

"Frank?" Slade's eyes scrunched up and he looked angry.

I patted Rambo on the chest. I slipped him my card and said, "You stay hiding now. Things might get dirty for a while. And you might think about a career change."

Rambo nodded like a junkie. "Already am, man. Already am."

"Get gone," I said.

Rambo jogged back into the Y.

I started for the car and Slade followed.

As we sat in rush hour traffic on the 5 freeway headed north, Slade lost his patience with my silence. "You going to tell me what the fuck, Frank? Let me in on the shit you know—it's only fair."

I pinched the bridge of my nose, rubbed my chin. After a few minutes I gave Slade my thoughts. "Celeste's dad is a high-profile lawyer—criminal defense."

"And?" Slade pounded his horn as a BMW cut us off. "You ain't getting nowhere faster, motherfucker. I hate people who drive BMWs. You know what kind of person—"

"And maybe Turner—or, better, Decassin—wanted Celeste's father to hear about the Jacoby family. Maybe Turner was supposed to pass along the information to scare Celeste's dad...But coming from Celeste. Like

214

planted information or something."

"That's some CIA shit."

"You think about it and…I don't know."

Slade snapped his fingers. "Wait, who the fuck was the lawyer for Jacoby. He was under investigation, right? So, whose his lawyer? If it's Celeste's daddy…"

"She'd know for sure. And tell daddy what she heard."

"There you go," Slade said.

"She fucking lied to me."

"That's batting a thousand. You know everybody lies."

I leaned back in my seat and shuddered. I saw her naked body again, those small shaking tits and the bored facial expression. I compared that to my vision of her from when I dropped her at home. She seemed small then—a child. "That girl played me, Skinny."

"Still doesn't explain the case of the gangster and his chopped off wang."

"Coincidence," I said, "in a manner of speaking."

"What?"

"You remember both Turner and Celeste said they go under the bridge a lot. To smoke. Fuck. Whatever. Whoever put Castaneda down there knew the body would be found, and maybe by Turner. By Regis Decassin's son…Or whatever he is."

Slade changed lanes and flipped off an older woman in a business suit. "You're saying it's pure coincidence they found a body that night?"

"On the same night Turner was passing a message through Celeste."

Slade thought for a long slow mile. "And we know the Castanedas worked for Decassin. I got that from a couple CIs. Well, not direct…But I'm pretty sure."

"Turner was passing a message," I said.

"And someone else was delivering a message to Decassin."

I nodded.

Slade added, "It was one hell of a message."

"So what we're saying then," I said looking out my window at the slow unraveling of strip malls and warehouses, "is that two messages were delivered in one night. That's what's confusing." We sat in silence for a few more miles and I thought about that: We had two messages being sent, both of those messages—also confusing—sent by and through the same person—Turner Malcolm. And Turner worked for his stepfather, Decassin. What that meant was Decassin was sending a message to Celeste's father and somebody was sending Decassin a message through Turner. But who? Who opposed Decassin? I rapped my knuckles on the window. "Who is it sending a message to Decassin, Slade? That's what we need to know."

"So, we're headed up there to ask the man."

I rolled down my window and breathed in some smog. "No. We're going to ask somebody else. We're going to trail them and ask the only way we know that'll get some answers."

"You talking about his hot ass wife?"

"Or the bodyguard," I said. "Whoever comes first."

Chapter 32

I didn't expect to get the bodyguard and the wife together, but that's what happened. Mid-evening, the late model Porsche slid through the gate and zoomed past us. The car accelerated onto the road and zipped out of sight. Slade was sleeping at the wheel—we were parked outside the gate beneath a stand of slow waving pine trees—and I was on watch. I slapped Slade's arm and said, "Let's go, Skinny. It's the wife and the security man."

Slade popped awake, started the car, and took off down the road. "Both of them in the same car?"

"You got it, partner."

Slade grunted and we followed the Porsche onto a southbound freeway entrance. The security man got in the fast lane and took it up to ninety. Slade followed about a quarter mile back. We weaved through light, post-rush-hour traffic. "You want me to pull them over? We could do it like that? Scare the two of them, if we want."

I didn't like that. Too many lies these past few days. Wherever these two went wouldn't be a lie—I'd see it with my own eyes. "No. Let's see what they're doing, where they're going."

The Porsche slid over after a few miles and exited at one of the downtown exits. Security man made a right down a one-way street and crept into Little Italy. The neighborhood was teeming with tourists and families out for weekend dinner.

Slade said, "You think they're eating out together?"

"Fuck if I know."

Slade pulled to the curb and flipped on his hazard lights.

The Porsche reached a valet stand and the teenage valet opened the door for Finney Portray. I whistled when she got out in a green slip dress so tight it looked like Spandex. Her hips swung as she moved to the curb followed by the security man. He wore a similar suit to when we first met him, off-gray with a nice tie and the slim bulge of a firearm beneath his armpit.

"Maybe he's the escort," I said.

But I was wrong. The security man slipped his arm around Finney and they walked into a restaurant called Limo's Hideaway. As they entered, security man's slim hand cupped Finney's plump ass.

Slade made a sound in his throat. "I hope you got money for the valet's tip, Frank." He flipped off the hazard lights and pulled through the intersection. We stopped in front of the valet stand.

"May I help you gentleman?" The hostess smiled at us and raised her eyebrows.

Slade said, "We're meeting some friends. A couple with a reservation for," Slade looked at his watch, "seven thirty-ish. Should be here already." He took out his cell and waved it. "Got a text from them."

"I don't have any four-person reservations for—"

"You know, we're only dropping in. A glass of bubbly and we're gone. They said we could—"

"Oh, you know what? I know where they are..." The hostess led us through the restaurant toward a cocktail area with a small, classy-looking bar and dark booths with leather seats. Limo's had the look of an old Italian place, though I could tell by the shine and sheen it was new. I figured it for a trendy place seizing on old world fare. I smelled pesto and gnocchi and my stomach growled. We found Finney and the security man in a corner booth. The young hostess bowed to them and presented us. "Your guests..." She turned and walked back to her posting.

I ignored the surprised look from our new friends and squeezed into the booth next to the security man. I put one big hand on the man's shoulder rig and said, "Let's just have a chat."

He relaxed and let his face go red. Finney didn't flinch.

Slade got in next to her and rubbed his hands together. "Where's the bread and butter? You order any vino yet?"

Cool as dry ice, Finney said, "Here comes the wine."

A white-shirted waiter opened a bottle of pinot noir and poured two glasses. "Shall I bring two more glasses?"

Slade said, "I'll take an old fashioned."

"Me too." When the waiter ran off, I said, "That stuff Italian?"

Slade laughed. "Pinot noir ain't Italian, Frank. You'll have to excuse my partner. He only recently joined the human race. He ran with the gorillas before that."

"This place is Italian. Seems to me you need to get some Italian wine if—"

"It's new world cuisine," Finney said and sipped from her glass. "Fusion food." Her eyes shined in the near dark. "They serve Italian wines, but I don't like them. Not even Prosecco."

"I'm a pro sicko, too. Aren't we all?"

Security man said, "The fuck do you two want now?"

"Don't believe we got your name?" Slade smiled.

"Jenson. Mayfair Jenson."

"Well, Mayfair," I tapped the gun beneath his coat, "first off, we want to know what the fuck this is." I looked from him to Finney, back again.

The waiter set our drinks on the table. "May I—"

"Later," Slade said and waved him back to the dining room.

Finney said, "You've never seen a case of infidelity, detectives?"

"Jesus H," Mayfair said under his breath.

"Oh, we've seen it." I put my elbows on the table, leaned down to sniff my cocktail. It was sweet and spicy. I bent and sipped without picking up the glass. "When I say 'what,' I happen to mean 'why'? A bit confusing, but even the dumbest among us can speak in riddles."

"I say what I mean," Finney said.

"I bet you do." Slade turned to get a better look at her. He scratched his cheek, let his hand slap against the table. "Did your husband kill the Jacoby family?"

Mayfair tensed, tried to reach across the table.

I pinned him with my arm and fat left thigh. "Let's

keep things civil. We just have a few questions and you can go back to wining and dining your boss's wife."

"I don't keep apprised of my husband's business dealings."

"Do you keep apprised of the murders of children?" I stared at her without blinking.

"No, I do not."

Mayfair groaned. "She doesn't have a goddamned thing to do with—"

"But I bet you know all about it," Slade said. He took a long swig from his cocktail and licked his lips. "I bet you watch the man's every move. That's how you can come out here and—"

"I'm a fucking errand boy."

"Long way from the Middle East," I said.

"Goddamn right about that."

"Please," Finney said, "I hate to hear about those ugly wars."

I looked at Mayfair and raised my eyebrows. "She don't support the troops?"

He shook his head and shrugged.

"Only when they stand at attention," Slade said while looking from Finney to Mayfair.

"Fuck you," Finney said.

"Tell us, Mayfair," I said, "you think the cuckolded drug czar killed the Jacoby family?" I kept my eyes on Finney while I spoke, hoped it pissed her off.

"I doubt it. And he's more like a...a lobbyist or something."

I rubbed my nose. "Lobbyist for who?"

"The cartel, dipshit." Finney smiled at me and sipped more wine.

"Which one?"

"Juarez." Mayfair and Finney said it at the same time.

"So honest," I said.

"So forthright," Slade said.

"Look," Mayfair turned to face me. "It's no secret what side Decassin is on. You two know this shit. And, yeah, me and Finney are..." He paused.

"We're fucking," she said and raised her pencil-thin eyebrows.

"Yeah," Mayfair continued, "and that's all there is on our end. That's it, okay?"

"Who killed the Castaneda brothers?"

"And who chopped off the one's wang?" Slade said.

"Gross." Finney sighed. "I lost my appetite."

Mayfair shook his head. "Look, the man doesn't let us in on his business. Like I said, I'm just a fucking errand boy."

"Me too," Finney said. "Just different errands."

I picked up my old fashioned, glared through the muddy liquid, put it to my lips and drank it down to ice cubes and sweat. "When's Turner coming back?"

"He's not," Mayfair said.

"Where's Decassin?"

Finney sighed again and said, "Probably fucking some whore at The Lady Shoppe."

"That dirty place off Rosecrans?" Slade sat up straighter.

Finney gave us each a bored look. "Are you two really that surprised?"

The waiter reappeared and said, "May I interest you in some appetizers?"

Chapter 33

As a cop—shit, former cop?—I'd seen my share of strip clubs. Been inside them. Fucked inside them. And I'd vomited inside them. Lots of people say they can't understand the allure. To them, I say it's the female body. Am I ashamed of that? I don't know—I can tell you it's a hell of a lot more civil than taking another person's life. I figured God knew about strip clubs. He made them, didn't He? The Lady Shoppe, though, was a bit different. Most cops knew or had a hunch that it was a way station for human smuggling. Not to mention porn and drugs and money laundering.

A year or so previous, the narco division did a raid and arrested ten strippers for peddling coke. Made the papers and local news shows. Thing was, the narcs wanted to turn one of the girls, get her to fold on the man who ran the place, a scummy Texan named Skooch McKinney. But none of the girls snitched, and Skooch knew how to hire lawyers.

Had the money for it, too.

The Lady Shoppe kept doing business, and the narcs kept punching the clock.

Slade parked the Ford on the street behind the

building. There was a gray door behind us and a red one up ahead. I decided the red door was the emergency exit for customers, and the gray door led into the back offices and the girls' dressing room, or undressing room.

Slade flipped the ignition and poked a cheek with his tongue. "You know they'll pat us down? No warrant, no entry. Skooch knows his rights—man's civically fucking engaged."

"It's always the scumbags," I said.

"You got to know how to get away with shit."

I nodded and watched my mirror. "We're going in the back way, Slade." I got out of the car and Slade followed. We crept along the building, close to the wall in hopes the security camera missed us, and stopped at the gray door.

Behind me, Slade said, "Well?"

I rapped on the door and made my voice a high-pitched warble. "I got locked out, baby! Let me in!" Nothing like a fat man talking like a parakeet. The door swung open and I caught a woman's slender, pedicured hand. "Hold on, sister."

I pushed her into the hallway and Slade closed the door behind us.

"What the fuck? Cops?" She tried to pull away—her brown hair swung across her almond-shaped eyes. "Let me go, asshole."

I gripped her wrist as tight as I could, knew my fingers would leave purple bruises. "First, I need you to tell me something."

"What?"

Skinny moved ahead of us down the hallway, stood in the darkness with his hand on his gun.

"Tell me if you've seen somebody."

"I've seen a lot of people."

"This guy looks like a Scarface wannabe, slick dresser and plastic surgery. He's Latino, and a high society type. I bet he throws money around."

"You're talking about Reg?"

"Am I?"

"The lobbyist, right?"

Slade looked back at us and shrugged.

I said, "Yeah, that's him."

"He's always here, in one of the private rooms." She tried to yank away again.

"How do we get there?"

"End of this hall and take a right. All the doors on your left are private. They should be locked though—good luck getting in." With her free hand, she adjusted her bra and pushed hair out of her eyes. "Don't fuck him up too bad, okay? He bought my kids Christmas presents last year."

I let her go and me and Slade moved down the hallway. "Yeah, well, tell them Santa might not make it down this year." The woman made an annoyed sound in her throat, opened a nearby door and went into a room. The door slammed. As me and Slade neared the hallway's end, the strip club's booming music echoed against the walls.

Slade peeked around the corner and lifted a hand. He turned and said, "Looks like the office."

I looked too and saw a square of light coming from a half-closed door. Filing cabinets and the corner of what I thought was a large safe. I lifted my chin in the other direction and we moved toward the private rooms. I put my ear to the first door and didn't hear anything.

225

Behind the second, I heard the bored moan of a woman and the grunts of a man I knew right away to be over-weight. Like me. I shook my head and we moved to the third door. Behind this one, I heard music—jazz. I turned to Slade and nodded. He moved in front of me and tried the door.

It wasn't locked.

We pushed the door open slowly. Against the far wall, on a twin bed with a floral print bedspread, Regis Decassin had his shirt off and his head pointed at the ceiling. His eyes were closed and a topless blonde woman in a pink G-string was giving him a blow job. Regis's torso was covered with prison and cartel tattoos: automatic weapons, Santa Muerte, Catholic crucifixes, and goateed faces of—I imagined—dead paisanos. He didn't hear us. Me and Slade stood together watching the woman's head move up and down. Decassin moaned once or twice and said, "That's right."

I removed my gun and held it with both hands.

Slade put both hands in his pockets and said, "Sing-ing telegram for Regis Decassin here."

"The fuck!"

"Oh, my god!" The girl twisted and fell back against the headboard.

"Stay there," I said.

Regis sat up and crossed his legs. He covered himself with the floral-patterned sheet. "I thought I told you to talk to my lawyer, you fucking—"

Slade sang in halfway decent soprano: "Your wife is fucking your bodyguard..."

Decassin didn't flinch. Instead, he sighed. "You think that's breaking news to me?"

I moved toward the bed. The girl was scared—she

didn't know a cop when she saw one. "Relax, sweet-heart," I said. "We're murder police. You can blow whoever you want. We don't give two shits. I'd advise you to ask for the money first."

She said, "I get half right away."

"Smart. Do me a favor. Get out of here."

She hopped off the bed and scooped up a pink sarong, draped it over her shoulders as she left the room. Slade moved after her and closed the door with a soft click.

With the quickness of a cat, Decassin swung his legs over the bed, tumbled onto the floor and came up with a little silver pistol. He lifted the gun in a long swinging arc and I squeezed my trigger twice. The rounds caught him in the lower left thigh and flesh tore like ground beef. He fell with a whomp sound.

The silver pistol clattered and slid to a stop near Slade who removed his hands from his pockets and picked up the gun. He inspected it carefully and said, "A little showpiece." I couldn't hear him clearly because my ears were ringing from the shots, but I read his lips.

I got a flashing vision of Santa Muerte in my head, the skeletal version I'd worshipped in the makeshift church. I swore I smelled candle wax and incense. But that was impossible. On the floor, Decassin whined. It sounded like it came through a steel pipe. The ring in my head died bit by bit, and I said, "I didn't want to shoot you."

Slade moved in front of me and squatted to stare Decassin in the face. "Who killed your enforcers, the Castanedas?" Slade waited, but he got no response. He took the silver pistol and pressed it into Decassin's mangled leg. Decassin screamed. Blood ran on the floor like sewage from an overflowing toilet. "You want to keep this up?" Slade pressed the pistol into the leg again and Decassin howled.

He got out a few words: "It was my wife."

"Like we said, she's out getting fucked by your body-guard."

"No," Decassin shivered and tried to scoot back against the wall. "She killed Enrico. Chato, too. Her and that fucking asshole, Mayfair. Last time I hire a veteran of a foreign fucking war."

I put my gun back in its holster and said, "Come again?"

"Her and Mayfair. They killed the Castanedas."

Slade said, "What the fuck for?" Regis started to fall unconscious and Slade prodded him with the pistol. "Why, motherfucker?"

Regis shivered. His eyes closed halfway and it was apparent the life was running out of him.

"He's done, Skinny."

Slade dug the pistol into Decassin's thigh. "You the one who killed the Jacoby family? Was it you, mother-fucker? You kill that little girl? Or did you have your goons do it?"

Decassin didn't answer. Couldn't answer.

Slade stood and shook his head. He turned to face me.

Somebody knocked on the door.

A squeaky voice in the hallway. "Sarah? Skooch said you should be done by now. I need this room for another client. You two still in there?"

Me and Slade looked at each other. He raised his

eyebrows—the fuck are we going to do? I took another look at Decassin's lifeless body and almost vomited. Well, shit. I moved toward the door and put my hand on the latch. As the woman knocked again, I swung the door inward and grabbed her wrist. She grunted as I yanked her inside and tossed her on the bed.

Slade closed the door and locked it.

"What the—oh, holy fuck." She paled when she saw Decassin and the floor slick with blood.

"Oh, my god. Please, please, please, leave me alone. I swear to god, I—"

Slade lifted the badge on the chain around his neck. "We're cops. Calm yourself."

"Cops did this?" Her hands went to her mouth, stifled a scream.

"Of course not," I said. "No cop would do this." Given my professional circumstances, it wasn't quite a lie. Or the truth. But you get away with whatever you can. Especially when it comes to murder. "We're looking for the guy who did it—you see anybody running out of here?"

"No, oh, god. Jesus. You two did this..." Again, she covered her mouth and her eyes filled with fear. She curled into the fetal position and began to cry.

"Frank, leave her. Forget it. We have to go..." He went to the door, unlocked it. "Now, Frank."

"She can ID us, Slade." I lifted the gun and instead of the girl I saw the bone-heavy face of Santa Muerte. I saw death and hatred. I saw Miranda's face emerge out of that, like she was resurfacing from deep waters. "She can tell who we are, Slade. She can—"

"Frank!" Slade's hand gripped my arm.

I lowered the gun and turned away from the girl.

Like pulling my eyes from Miranda's bruised and water-bloated body. Fuck. Slade tugged on me. We were in the hallway a moment later, Slade slinking along one wall. Me, huffing along the other. As we reached the corner, where another hallway lead to the back exit, the office door creaked open and poured yellow light.

"What the fuck?"

"Go," Slade said and ran toward the door.

I started after him and heard more shouting. A gunshot rang over my left ear and plunged into the wall above Slade's left shoulder. We both crouched and sprinted faster.

"Stop, you assholes!"

Slade plunged through the door and into the dark evening.

Another shot sounded, this one near my right ear, and slammed into the door jamb.

When I made it outside, I realized I was holding my breath and opened my mouth. Damp air ran into my throat and lungs. Slade was already in the Ford. I collapsed into the passenger seat and the car's engine strained as Slade pressed the throttle to the floor.

In the rearview mirror I saw a pudgy white man in a black ten-gallon hat emerge from the strip club's rear exit. He waved a pistol in the air and flipped us the bird.

"Mission accomplished," I said.

Slade didn't look at me. After we merged onto the freeway headed downtown, he found his words. "I sure hope I get assigned the Decassin murder. Otherwise, we're fucked."

Chapter 34

We stopped at a dive bar near the airport.

We both ordered tequila on ice. I couldn't hold my glass. My hands shook too much. The bartender left us alone. He understood the look on my face. A don't fuck with me look. Not tonight, motherfucker.

Slade kept fingering his badge, twirling it on the chain and letting the chain unspool.

When the tequila started working its way into me, I spoke. "He had a weapon, lifted it and came at me with it. You know, if I was on duty...I swear to fuck that's a legal shooting."

"Except we walked in on him getting a knob job."

"So the fuck what?"

"We got two strippers with eyes on us..." Slade's hand shook as he sipped. The ice in his glass chimed like dinner bells. "The Texan, too..."

"Those strippers won't say shit. The Texan neither. Man wouldn't admit he twice missed a target as fat as me. A real Texan would be ashamed of himself."

"I guess that's true."

The paradox of a murder detective killing a murder suspect did not escape me. I squinted hard and drank faster. "Fuck Decassin. He might not have pulled the trigger on the Castanedas, but he was as dirty as it gets."

Slade said, "And those brothers, they probably killed more people than you and me have ever seen dead."

"It's true."

"What bothers me is this Jacoby thing. I ain't seen shit about it in the news. We give it to this fed—well, two of them—and it vanishes like a fucking white rabbit."

I nodded.

Slade said, "That's got to be tied to Applewhite. And the girl's dad, what's her name?"

"Celeste Richards."

"Right, her lawyer daddy. You got two lawyers involved here, one of them running for county DA. And you got this whole stadium thing downtown. I mean, what the fuck?"

"We're as far from an answer as when we started."

"You remember…" Slade stopped and finished his tequila. The bartender poured us each a new one, moved back down the bar and leaned into a dough-faced woman's ear. "You remember how before we caught the woman delivering the boots, you said it was Applewhite, people like him? They always did it. It always came back to them."

"Yeah."

"And we got Applewhite's car—the Juarez decal on the back window—spotted at the second Castaneda killing. We got Finney Portray double-crossing her husband."

"Yeah, that's right."

"And we got the two feds not doing a fucking thing.

Least of all not interviewing Decassin."

"It's a bad look to interview the man running a PAC for the DA candidate."

"Maybe," Slade said, "you've been right. And more right than even you know."

I shrugged. "I guess, in an indirect way, there's some way of saying how—"

"And Jackson suspends you," Slade said nodding to himself. "Jackson fucking suspends you."

"He was mad about us interviewing Applewhite."

Slade laughed and drank, licked his bottom lip. "You were right about this, Frank."

I didn't know how to respond. All this sounded like a hamster chasing his own tail.

"It's somebody with power, Frank. Above Applewhite. Fuck Applewhite. He's in it, sure. But the feds letting a triple murder stay in the red? You remember what Chato said? When he came to ID his brother?"

"He said a bunch of stuff."

"No, something about how only a white man runs things over here."

"Shit." I sighed and rubbed my neck. "And Applewhite's half-Mexican."

"You got it," Slade said.

We sat there for a few minutes without speaking. The bartender poured us another round. I drank and thought I might ask Slade to drop me off near the Santa Muerte shrine. Something inside pulled at me, kept yanking and yanking me back to the place. Like I wanted to fall at Santa Muerte's feet again. Yet another fucking thing I didn't understand. It lurked in my head, like a hunch on a case. One of those dumb luck things you think to try because...Well, why the fuck not? My hands had stopped shaking and I studied my fingers. Same fingers that held the gun and shot Regis Decassin to pieces.

Slade's voice sounded hollow. "If Applewhite's half-Mexican, that means somebody else is part of this thing. It's got to be somebody…"

"Somebody bigger," I said. "More important."

"More powerful."

"Twisted as fuck."

"To get the feds to shut up, to get Jackson on your ass, and to keep it all out of the papers…"

I finished my tequila. "Like always, it's some gangster in a suit. A tailored suit."

Slade stood and shook out his arms. He adjusted the badge against his chest and shrugged. "Looks like we need to keep going, partner. I can't see any other way."

"Fuck it," I said. "Where to next?"

"Tomorrow morning we're going to have a chat with Xander Dames."

"Sounds good, Skinny. Hey, you mind dropping me a couple blocks off Market Street?"

"I guess so, Frank. As long as you promise to get some sleep."

"I'll sleep," I said. "Like the dead."

Chapter 35

Slade dropped me near Market Street and I walked a block past the Salvation Army, found the gray building with the security door and keypad. The night air was cool against my skin and I felt at home in the slanting darkness of the city. I didn't know the punch code to enter the Santa Muerte shrine, so I leaned against the wall and waited.

Across the street three homeless men were huddled up together outside a mechanic's shop. They lay in twisted sleeping bags, puffs of cigarette smoke rising above them every few seconds. The street was empty besides that. After forty minutes or so, I heard footsteps down along the sidewalk and echoing between the buildings. Sounded like high heels. Sure enough, a few seconds later a slim woman in a pant suit and heels shuffled across the sidewalk and approached. I cleared my throat and put my hands behind my back. The woman saw me when she crossed through the parking lot and she stopped. It was Vera, the woman I met my first time at the shrine.

"Hello, Detective. I'm surprised to see you again."

"Why's that?"

She came to the door and looked at me sideways. "I thought you'd go back to confession and mention worshipping a false idol."

"That's the thing…What if the lady isn't false?"

Vera punched in the door's code and I followed her into the dark, humid hallway.

We walked in stride to the room where the Santa Muerte figure sat bathed in candlelight. Vera said, "There she is."

"You think she's on the side of good or evil?"

Vera walked down the aisle between the chairs. I followed. When we got to the front of the room, I fell to one knee and lowered my head. Vera stood above me and said, "I think Santa Muerte knows that evil depends on who is good."

"I don't know what you mean."

"Are you a good man, Detective?"

I heard Decassin's screams and saw blood wash behind my eyes. "Not always."

"Some days you're evil, and some days you're good."

I said, "Usually, I'm evil in the nights."

Vera nodded and kneeled beside me. "Whatever side you're on," she said, "Santa Muerte is looking over your shoulder. She's riding with you."

"Seems better than Jesus or the Holy Spirit."

"Do you think the evil you see in your work is because people themselves are evil?"

I stared at the candlelight flickering off Santa Muerte's bones. Maybe we're like fire—it can be a force for evil or a force for good. Or was that too simple? Too stupid? "I don't know," I said. "I'm not sure if people are evil. I think we—all of us—can do some shitty things. That's about as far as my philosophy goes."

Vera didn't say anything else to me.
But we did pray together.

Chapter 36

The challenge getting into FBI headquarters to see Xander Dames came down to one thing: We didn't have an appointment with him and he didn't answer our phone calls or return our messages. We thought about entering the building and trying to find his office, but Slade didn't want to risk his job. I knew I'd be stopped long before I got to speak to Dames. What we did is sit around and wait for him to leave the building.

Slade bought a New York Times and sat at a bus stop across the street, pecking at the crossword with his pencil. The rest of the paper sat in a pile beside him. Every so often, if nobody else was at the stop, Slade waved an approaching bus onward by shaking his head and pointing up the street with his thumb. I took a post outside the building. I leaned against one of the office park coffee kiosks and looked at images of the Castaneda bodies on my cell. The FBI headquarters shared a building downtown with a host of other federal agencies. We didn't look too suspicious, I hoped. Just your everyday city cops staking out a federal agent. By mid-morning, I began to think that Dames might not appear. In fact, I felt stupid standing there and waiting for an agent who, for all we knew, could be chasing down a lead somewhere.

Slade disagreed.

I called him on my cell and watched him put down the crossword and answer. "What now, Frank?"

"What if he's not here?"

"He's here. Or the woman is. One of them is here."

"How do you know?"

"Because, Frank, not everybody is trying to clock in and go down to the local dive bar. You know, like a city cop? Most people work for a living and, surprise, they really fucking work."

I flipped him off. "You know, technically, I'm working for free right now."

"The fuck you are. You're suspended with pay."

"It's reduced," I said.

"Well, Frank. I'm sorry you have to do some actual fucking detective work."

I shook my head and thought about hanging up on him.

Slade said, "Frank?"

"Yeah?"

"Is that the woman agent? Look, she's coming down the steps."

I twisted my head and saw a short woman in tight slacks jogging out of the building. Short bobbed hair, a dark long-sleeved blouse and the fast walk of a born athlete. "Fuck, that's her."

Slade said, "You're on her first. I'm right behind you."

When you're big, like me, people remember you. Though I met Tracy Atkins once, I knew she'd remember me for my size. I followed about a half block behind her as she weaved through the street crowds. She walked fast and I imagined she had a meeting in one of the hotel bars or numerous lounges. I knew Slade was right behind me, but I wasn't sure he marked Atkins as clear as I did. I didn't want to lose her so I started to jog. As I did, she turned into the downtown Marriott and nodded at the bellman as he held the door. The same bellman held the door when I approached and I handed him a dollar bill. He smirked at me. Inside the hotel, I crossed through the check-in area and into a sunken lounge area with big oak tables and luxurious leather couches. I stopped for a moment to search for Atkins. I saw her at the bar in the lounge's far corner. She waved down the barman and spoke to him for a few seconds. He sauntered off to make Atkins a drink. I sat down on the nearest couch. Atkins spun on her barstool and surveyed the lounge and lobby area. I hunched down and pretended like I was reading a menu. When Atkins turned back to the bar, I called Slade. "She's hanging at the bar. I think it's just lunch time. You want me to stay on her?"

"Yeah, let's wait. I want to think for a second."

We hung up and I leaned back into the couch, crossed one leg over the other. A cocktail waitress approached. I waved her off. The barman brought Atkins a flute of champagne and she sipped it with slow and deliberate poise. Drinking on the job, huh? A second later, Slade called me. "What's up? What are you thinking?"

"I'm wondering if I should go back to sit on Dames?"

To me, that sounded right. "It's probably best. I'll watch Atkins eat her Cobb salad and head back to meet you—that sound like a plan?"

Slade didn't answer.

"Slade? That sound like a plan?"

"Frank," he said, "do yourself a favor."

"What's that?"

"Don't do anything until I get in there."

"What are you talking about?"

And then Ronald J. Applewhite walked right past me in a pinstriped suit and neon pink tie. He tapped Atkins on the shoulder, gave her a peck on the cheek, and slid onto a barstool. "Fuck, man." I didn't believe it.

Slade said, "I'm crossing the street now."

Slade sat next to Atkins and I took the barstool next to Applewhite. As we sat down, Slade said, "You two look cute together."

Applewhite let a big breath seep out from between his lips. "You two fucks again? What do I have to do to get you to cool it? Don't you two know any goddamn thing about pay grade?"

I waved at the barman. "Cold beers for me and my partner here." The barman poured two draft beers and set them in front of me and Slade. I took a long sip and left the white froth on my mouth. "Yeah," I said. "We know all about it. We know all about a wannabe DA in bed with a drug trafficker too. Lots to know in this big old world."

Slade said, "What we can't figure is what Agent Atkins here has to do with all this. Other than covering up the Jacoby murder with that partner of hers. What's his name?" Slade snapped his fingers a couple times.

Atkins said, "Xander doesn't have shit to do with

this. He's back at the office looking at DNA results right this minute."

Applewhite nudged her. "These fucks don't deserve to know anything. They can't do shit."

I swiveled on my barstool and faced Applewhite. I leaned into him so he could feel my weight on his torso and right thigh. "Maybe you forgot we're murder police, Applewhite."

"Not you, Pinson," he said. "You're not even police at all. Not anymore."

"Well, looky-look at this…" Slade was tapping at his cell phone. "Special Agent Atkins here did a juris doctorate at Jefferson." He squinted at his screen. "Says here you wanted to get into politics. Is that right?"

"I graduated top of my class."

"Good for you," I said. "What's all this got to do with—"

"She's networking with the next DA, Frank," Slade said. "I'm guessing she's looking for some kind of special appointment. Something she can make her political bones on, but something that can't be fucked up. Hell, it'll look pretty good for a former FBI agent to run for state senator."

Applewhite said, "You're getting ahead of yourself, Ryerson."

"Am I though?"

"I don't give two fat fucks about your career trajectory, Atkins," I said. "What I do give a fuck about, and I give lots of fucks about this, are the three dead bodies we found in the desert. We want to know how they got there. And we want to know who did it."

Neither Atkins nor Applewhite said a damn thing.

"Well," Slade said, "I guess me and Frank need to

make a stop at the Tribune newsroom." He looked at the time on his cell. "Plenty of room for this to make tonight's print deadline. They'll have it up online around this evening I expect. They'll want to beat the TV news."

"What's the story?" Applewhite sipped his vodka martini.

"Local DA and regional FBI office collaborate on not giving a shit about a triple murder."

"You think Jacoby was an innocent?"

"No," I said, "but his daughter and wife were."

"The wife was as dirty as her husband."

"The girl then." I leaned into him more, finished my beer with one big gulp.

"Look," Applewhite said, "you want to know who killed the Jacoby family? It wasn't me...I don't have that in me. Jesus, what do you think I am?"

"You ordered it done," I said.

Slade said, "Fucking A, right."

Atkins bowed her head.

Applewhite shook his head and used one hand to point a finger at the ceiling.

"What's that supposed to fucking mean?" God, that anger came up in me at that second. I wanted to bite the finger off his hand, shoot him in the face.

"I'm just a foot soldier in all this shit."

I removed my pistol from its snug holster and shoved it into his ribs.

"Jesus, Frank," Slade said.

Applewhite grunted and said, "You're fucking insane."

"Let's say I'm exploring who the fuck I'm faithful to."

Atkins made a move for her gun, but Slade had his own gun in her belly before she could get there. "Nada, señorita," he whispered.

I shoved the gun deeper into Applewhite. "Give us something to go on. And, yeah, we'll go to the press. But we might—no, I might—try and do worse."

Atkins said, "Talk to Decassin's wife, assholes."

Slade made a sound with his lips. "Finney Portray?"

I bent over the bar and met Slade's gaze.

Applewhite said, "We're all dead."

I put my gun away and finished Applewhite's martini for him. "That's true," I said, "eventually."

Chapter 37

Slade exited the freeway and headed west toward the housing development where we first met Finney Portray. I thought about the raised eyebrows she gave me that night, her feigned annoyance at us being there. The way she tilted her champagne flute to her lips, a perfect statue sipping the nectar of life. And to think Decassin sat there all high and mighty, looking like Napoleon on a fucking plush throne. I didn't know what to expect when we confronted Portray, but I kept hoping—somewhere deep inside myself—for Atkins and Applewhite to prove liars.

Slade said, "You really think this woman is behind all this death?"

"I don't know, Skinny. Would it be a surprise?"

"Man, nothing fucking surprises me anymore."

"That's the truth," I said. "Every second you turn around—it's a fucking surprise."

Slade nodded and said, "Frank, I want to say I'm sorry about the way this went. I don't know why it is that Jackson did you so wrong. And this thing you told me about Miranda. I mean, shit Frank. I'm sorry about it and...I don't know what I can say."

I touched my sore face and winced. Johnny's brass knuckles left their mark. I said, "You've done me right all the way through, Skinny. What we need to do right now is solve this fucking thing. We need to put it behind us." And I decided then—without a second thought—to put my hate for Johnny behind me. Or to pretend it didn't exist. There were worse evils in the world.

We crested a hill and descended through a cool section of road with golf course ponds on each side. It was still bright out this early in the afternoon and I enjoyed the brief moment of cold air. Up ahead, the guard kiosk sat with the big wrought-iron gate behind it. Slade pulled the car up to the same plump guard with his polo shirt and the senseless grin on his face. Slade rolled down his window.

The guard said, "Can I help you gentlemen?"

Slade nodded. "You can open the gate without giving us a bunch of shit."

I removed my gun and held it on my lap where the guard could see it. "And you can make sure not to call anybody when we pass through."

The guard hesitated for an instant. I shifted in my seat to face him. That was all it took. He turned and entered the kiosk. A moment later the wrought-iron gate slid open and Slade drove forward onto the pristine black asphalt of the country club.

We rolled slowly down the streets, both of us taking in the pleasant yet antiseptic sight of mission-style tract homes. The lawns were bright green and all the flowers were in a state of perpetual bloom. A few older men in golf carts passed us in the opposite direction. We got kind waves and smug smiles. In a way, it was nice— maybe that was the biggest problem I had with it.

"Fucking postcard living," Slade said.

"Don't let it fool you. These motherfuckers here are just as dirty as your average street pimp, your run-of-the-mill drug dealer. Maybe dirtier. Everybody shits from the same place, and it always smells. A fat bank account ain't perfume."

Slade's mouth turned down at the corners. He swung us around a long curve and pulled the Ford to the curb outside Decassin's house. No pleasant sounds of jazz or sprinklers today. Only the rush of blood in my ears.

We walked to the front door and Slade rang the doorbell.

A middle-aged white woman with a pinched-up face answered the door.

"Is Mrs. Portray here?"

"Upstairs—I'm the housekeeper. You want me to get her?"

Slade revealed his badge. "I'm a homicide detective, miss. I'm just here to ask her some questions. She knows me, and I'm supposed to meet her this afternoon."

"Come in, detectives. Please."

We passed into the foyer and the woman nodded at me. I didn't have my badge to show her. It was a blessing she didn't ask.

She said, "I'll just go and let Finney know you're here."

We nodded and watched the woman climb a nearby staircase.

"It's going to feel nice to use my cuffs," Slade said.

"I bet."

We stood there in silence, both of us staring at the expensively decorated room. Lots of modern art and huge vases with fake sticks poking out of them. What an odd way to live, all this well-planned crap everywhere. It reminded me of a movie set, though I'd never been near one.

From the floor above, we heard a sharp crack—like a balloon popping. Slade led the way up the stairs, both of us moving cautiously and with our guns drawn.

When we reached the landing, there was a rush of movement to our right. Somebody moving into a room. The hallway stretched in both directions. I saw two doors opposite each other on the left. I leaned into Slade's ear and said, "Let me clear those rooms." He nodded. I crested the landing with Slade covering me to the right and prodded open the nearest door. It was a bathroom and it was empty. The other door led to a study with a big oak desk and a bunch of Aztec masks and other artifacts. Decassin would never enjoy those again. I wondered what would happen to them. The study was also empty. I moved out into the hall behind Slade and we slunk forward toward the two doors on the other side of the staircase. We reached the first bedroom and took up positions on each side.

Slade said, "It's the police! Get on the ground and put your weapons on the floor!"

A hushed flurry of gunshots came through the door and smacked the wall between us. I felt the wind from the rounds rush past my face. I looked at Slade and his eyes told me what I needed to hear. I threw my shoulder into the door and it collapsed. I fell with it, all the wood crunching beneath me like balsa—I landed on my right shoulder, felt something sharp enter my knee. There were more of those soft-popping gunshots and I realized my gun was beneath my bulk. I shifted to my other side and, as I lifted my head, I saw Slade slide into the room like a shadow.

He fired two shots from his 9 mm, torch-like blasts that rung in my ears.

Mayfair Jenson fell against the bed, all his red-black blood coloring the white bedspread. He looked at me when he toppled over, his beady eyes dead-black even in the bright afternoon light coming through the window. I got to my knees and Slade moved deeper into the room, pried a Glock from Mayfair's hand and slid it back toward me. He looked out the large open window and shook his head. "She's running," he said. "Stay here, Frank." Before I could protest, Slade ran out of the room and I heard his footsteps fading down the stairs. I got up and double-checked that Mayfair was gone. I put my fingers to his jugular and he had a slight, irregular pulse. Slade plugged him three times in the center of his chest—all textbook kill shots. I noticed the bathroom door and quickly opened it, my gun drawn. The woman with the pinched-up face was in the bathtub, dead from a bullet in the right temple. I closed her eyes with my palm and, in the bedroom, walked to the open window.

I saw Finney Portray sprinting across the green blanket of the golf course. She must have slid down the house's red tile roof and hopped onto the grass. She wore blue panties, but nothing else. In her right hand, she carried what I now know was a shotgun. About thirty yards behind her, his gun trained on Finney, Slade jogged and shouted for her to stop and drop the gun. She stumbled and fell, climbed to her feet without looking back at Slade. On the fairway, a golf cart with two old men stopped and they got off, stared at the near-naked woman running with the shotgun. She passed in front of them without stopping. Slade kept shouting. About twenty yards past the golf cart, Finney Portray stopped and turned to face Slade.

He stopped running, but kept walking toward her, his gun raised and steady.

Finney's face looked dark with the sun starting to sink low in the west—that big source of natural light right behind her. Her naked breasts rose and fell with her rapid breathing. She held the shotgun at her side, and I knew if she pointed it at Slade he'd kill her. Like he did Mayfair.

But Finney Portray didn't point the gun at Slade.

Instead she bent to her knees, flipped the gun with cool and effortless precision—the barrel came to rest directly against her chin—and Finney Portray squeezed the trigger.

Chapter 38

I spent the next day installing my new toilet, an American Standard.

It felt good to sweat and get something done for once.

And I was sick and tired of pissing into a hole. When I finished, I sat in my living room drinking cold bottles of beer and thinking with some joy about my dead wife. I was waiting for the evening news report—Slade sent me a text message saying I should watch it. My bladder got full and I pissed in the new toilet.

I was proud of the way it flushed and refilled with water.

I had another beer and the news program started. A good-looking brunette with too much makeup did most of the talking. The gist: A couple high society types wound up dead over the weekend, a prominent political gatekeeper and his stunning wife. It looked to detectives like the wife went nuts and killed the husband, a trusted security colleague, and a domestic employee. Lead detective on the case, one Slade "Skinny" Ryerson, approached the woman at her country club estate— oddly, not named in the report—and she killed herself in spectacular fashion. Detectives believed the wife, with an accomplice, was also responsible for the murder of two other people in her husband's employ—Enrico Frederico Pablo Castaneda and his twin brother, José Carlos, affectionately known on the streets as Chato. Not a mention about the Jacoby family. The wife's motives had to do with her husband's sexual indiscretions.

That was it.

Nothing about Applewhite or the FBI either.

They followed with a brief story about a veteran city police detective getting suspended on suspicion of assault. They showed the brief clip of me smacking Johnny with my pistol. No charges filed—just the video for proper embarrassment.

I drank two more beers and popped a third. That's when I called Slade.

He didn't sound happy. "They fucking lied about everything."

"Not everything," I said. "Some of it's true."

"Just enough."

"Did you know that's how they'd do us?"

Slade groaned. "Nope. Should have figured though."

"We still don't know why Portray killed the Jacoby family. Or why she had it done."

"I can't imagine she did it herself," Slade said.

"But Mayfair Jenson—he knew how to kill."

Slade grunted agreement. "We still don't know the why. Why kill them? I know it has something to do with the stadium plan and—"

"A plan that's now dead."

"Right, but did that kill it?"

"If not, it's sure as shit dead now." I thought for a minute and finally said, "We know anything about Finney Portray's family?"

I heard Slade shuffling some papers and opening his notebook. He searched for a minute and said, "Mother, RN at Mercy. Works on the pediatric floor. Father, let's see, ooh. Too bad about all this. Man's a pastor here in the city. Runs a church off Broadway. It's called—"

"New Life Church," I said. It hit me then—I remembered Slade ripping the flier off the telephone pole. The night before they did Chato in the same part of the city. "We were supposed to run over there, Slade. You remember that flier?"

More shuffling and Slade said, "Fuck me. I got it right here."

"I bet, you take a close look, the man's church is in the part of the city was supposed to get bought and sold. Where they were going to sell the property to P&J Associates for pennies on the dollar."

Slade chuckled. "And there it is…"

"Finney Portray killed herself—and had the Jacoby family killed—to protect mommy and daddy."

"And New Life Church," Slade said.

I pushed air through my teeth while thinking about it. "Could be the lawyer for Mark Jacoby figured out who killed his client. Decassin got nervous and—even though it was his wife's doing—tried to remind the lawyer what was at stake. He was sending a message through Celeste Richards."

"Telling the lawyer to keep quiet, or his little girl was on the hit list."

"But killing the two brothers…"

Slade said, "Not Decassin. No—I'd bet a month's pay that it was Applewhite's idea. Him and Finney Portray. The brothers probably knew about the Jacoby killings. Or, hell, they were in on it. Just another example of the evil eating their own. Applewhite and Portray cleaning up a fucking mess."

"Forget the murders," I said. "Fuck—they got to an FBI agent. A city police captain. And Applewhite is baby-ass clean. The fucker is going to be the DA."

"And nobody will say shit after all these bodies. Man, you think about it like this and it runs together. In a crazy way, it's logical."

"But senseless. And we don't have it all. We still don't know who it is pushing Applewhite to the DA spot. I mean, who's the gangster in the tailored suit?"

Slade said, "I don't think we'll ever get it."

We hung up and I thought about the case for a long hour. It was appalling how fast one act of hatred—trying to take something that doesn't belong to you—spiraled into a series of murders and betrayals. Appalling, sure.

But not surprising.

That night, when I was good and drunk, I wandered down to a tattoo parlor on the corner. The place smelled like reefer and gun oil. Hip-hop played on invisible speakers. I went up to the front desk and a burly guy with big silver gauges in his earlobes shook my hand. "What can we do for you tonight? I'm Robin."

"Hey, Robin," I said. "I'm looking to get a little work done—my first tattoo."

"No shit. What are you thinking?"

I removed my shirt and traced the outline of a necklace across my chest. The folds of my belly jiggled as I talked. "A rosary," I said, "all the way around my neck. Like it's real."

"I can do it tonight," he said.

"But I don't want the Virgin. No. What I want to know is, can you do Santa Muerte?"

Robin smiled and gold inserts glinted between his teeth. "Can I do Santa Muerte? I fucking love to do Santa Muerte. If we start now, I can finish before midnight."

My chest and neck burned with pain as I walked downtown toward Market Street. I stopped in a corner store and bought some small bottles of whiskey, slugged them down to dull the pain. It didn't work. I pulled out my cell and dialed my daughter's number. The phone rang three times and I heard her voice.

"Daddy?"

"I can't wait," I said.

"For what?"

"The baby."

"Me neither," Kimmie said. "Will you be here? When it comes?"

"You're goddamn right I will."

"Good night, Daddy." Kimmie hung up.

"Good night," I said to the dial tone.

Another cool, dry night in the city. I listened for sirens, but heard none. I turned south and, after a block and a half, reached the gray building where I planned to honor and pray to Santa Muerte. I walked across the parking lot with long, lumbering steps. I shuddered with pain as my shirt rubbed against the ink injected below the surface of my skin. When I got to the security door I didn't have to wait like I did the previous night.

Vera trusted me.

She gave me the code.

ACKNOWLEDGMENTS

I wish to thank my family for their continued support of my writing and art—thanks to my wife, Lesley, and my little son, Charlie. Sorry for spending so much time at the keyboard! And thanks, as always, to Chris Rhatigan and the publishing team at All Due Respect and Down & Out Books. So proud of this one!

MATT PHILLIPS lives in San Diego. His books include *The Rule of Thirds, You Must Have a Death Wish, Countdown, Know Me from Smoke, Accidental Outlaws, The Bad Kind of Lucky,* and *Three Kinds of Fool.* More info at MattPhillipsWriter.com.

On the following pages are a few
more great titles from the
Down & Out Books publishing family.

For a complete list of books and to
sign up for our newsletter,
go to DownAndOutBooks.com.

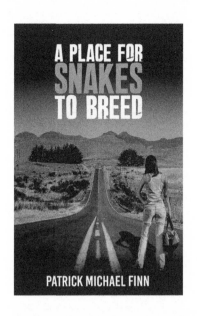

A Place for Snakes to Breed
Patrick Michael Finn

Down & Out Books
June 2021
978-1-64396-207-8

The desert spares no souls.

Set in the scorched and unforgiving deserts of the American Southwest, *A Place for Snakes to Breed* follows Weldon Holt's desperate search for his daughter Tammy, who is lost in the vicious landscape of interstate truck stop prostitution and its nightworlds "where the fruit of human trade is harvested by razor blades and cheap pistols."

Avenging Angelenos
A Sisters in Crime/Los Angeles Anthology
Sarah M. Chen, Wrona Gall, and
Pamela Samuels Young, editors

Down & Out Books
June 2021
978-1-64396-204-7

With an introduction by Frankie Y. Bailey and eleven original stories by Avril Adams, Paula Bernstein, Hal Bodner, Jenny Carless, LH Dillman, Gay Toltl Kinman, Melinda Loomis, Kathy Norris, Peggy Rothschild, Meredith Taylor, and Laurel Wetzork.

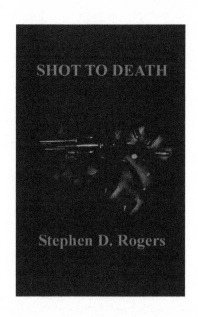

Shot to Death
31 Crime Stories
Stephen D. Rogers

All Due Respect, an imprint of
Down & Out Books
April 2021
978-1-64396-193-4

Thirty-one bullets that will leave you gasping for breath...

From hardboiled to noir to just plain human, these stories allow you to experience lives you escaped, and to do so with dignity, humor, and an eye toward tomorrow.

Houses Burning and Other Ruins
William R. Soldan

Shotgun Honey, an imprint of
Down & Out Books
May 2021
978-1-64396-115-6

In this gritty new collection, one bad choice begets another, and redemption is a twisted mirage. The troubled characters that inhabit the streets and alleys of these stories continually find themselves at the mercy of a cold, indifferent world as they hurtle downward and grapple for hard-won second chances in a life that seldom grants them.